I'VE GOT A MYSTERY IN MY POCKET

David Booker

Table of Contents

Contributions by Ian Walker on Murder at Mildenhall

Dedicated to
Dorothy Sayers whose books started me on my love of
detective fiction.

MURDER AT MILDENHALL
DETAILS

OSI Agent Oliver was half sitting half lying over his desk. He rubbed his eyes and tried to bring everything back into focus. In front of him was a pile of shredded material he had spent hours trying to piece together. Elbows on the desk, fingers intertwined supporting his chin, Agent Oliver stared at the shredded computer disk. Even with tweezers and more than one high powered magnifying glass he had been having a hard time and now his neck hurt as well as his back. His eyes struggled to remain open. In six hours he had made very little headway. Frustrated and fatigued he was ready to admit defeat.

He placed all the clipped material into an envelope and walked into his supervisor's office. "Logan I'm having a hell of a time with this, Is there any way you'd let me bring these to Harry. This is right up his alley." Logan reached for the envelope and peered inside. He was about to pour them onto his desk when Oliver stayed his hand. "Better not touch them. The oil in your hands will make it harder to read if we ever do get them together." Oliver retrieved the envelope as Logan reached into a side drawer and pulled out a leave slip. "Will fourteen days be enough do you think?" Logan poised his pen as he waited for Oliver's response. "Sure" he attempted to take the slip but Logan held it fast. "Head on over to the Commanders office for his signature, while you're on your way I'll call him so he knows what it's for." He picked up the phone as Oliver headed out the door.

Logan called him back. "Why don't you try again to get Harry to cross train? I could have him under our wing in an hour. What's a brilliant computer person doing coming in as a cook anyways?" Oliver sat on the arm of a chair. "He was slated for Tactical Communications but got taken out for a congenital defect, no depth perception. He was given a choice of Butcher or Cook and chose Cook. Then when Services found out about his skills, they made him their computer specialist. Lucky for us he kept his Secret rating. I'll get him going on this. I bet it will only take him a couple of days."

Harry yawned and placed his feet on the pulled out bottom desk drawer. Lazily he watched the disk and tape drives shunting data back and forth accomplishing the backup. He found humor in the fact that he was a cook yet was assigned as a computer administrator which was far outside his training and duties. The computer aspects were interesting to him but he found the mountains of paperwork a pain. The Wang VS100 he was working on now looked impressive to the unenlightened, but he was well aware of how antiquated the system was even for 1986! The only part of the job that gave him any fulfillment was figuring out the various problems that came up. He was an analyst at heart and had kept careful track of all problems and solutions. Some of his notes he sent to Headquarters to assist other administrators when there was something major.

The noise in the small office space was deafening but he was used to it. He could almost shut out the noise at will, always supposing he didn't actually go deaf first. The door slowly opened behind him. The sound was lost in the hammer blows of an impact printer. The chatter of the drives added to the general clamor. Harry jumped as a heavy hand was laid on his shoulder. He spun around to see the smiling face of Agent Oliver grinning like a Cheshire cat." Damn it Oliver, I damn near crapped my pants!"

"Outside," Oliver mouthed pointing with his thumb toward the hallway. As the thick door shut behind them the sudden quiet was a relief. "That's better," laughed Oliver pulling out a pack of cigarettes and passing one to Harry. "We need your help again" he remarked as he lit their cigarettes. Harry grumbled bitterly. "I thought you OSI folks had people to do this work, why pick on me?" "It's detail work" Oliver said patting Harry's shoulder, "It's a lot of detail work and we know how much you love detail work."

Harry took a long drag at the Dunhill and let the smoke out slowly. He held his nose and popped his ears to get them clear again. "What kind of details." He asked. Oliver held out a sealed envelope in a paper bag. "We have a shredded disk, we need you to piece it back together and see if it can be read. If it is readable give me a call and we'll take over, think you can handle it?" Harry took the proffered leave slip and glanced over it. "Two weeks and signed by the Base Commander? You guys are serious! I'll start on it as soon as I get home." Oliver ground out his cigarette. "The sooner the better, pal."

SO IT BEGINS

Setting the rest of the backup on auto he made his way to the manager's office and placed the leave paper on the desk. "This is the third leave in six months!" Mr. Lawrence barked irritated. "Do you want to explain what this one's for?" Harry shook his head, "Sorry boss, no can do." Mr. Lawrence motioned as if he was going to tear it up. "Before you do that, you might notice it already has been approved. I suggest you take a look at the signature."

His superior raised an eyebrow at the sight of the Base Commander's scrawl and handed the third copy to Harry. "See you in two weeks but try and be available if we need you, nobody else understands these damn machines." Harry spoke as he headed out the door. "Sorry but if you remember I did ask for an assistant, what is it now three months ago, what would you do if I dropped down dead?"

Dropping the envelope securely into the glove box of his car he drove to his house, courtesy of the OSI. He was the best computer expert at Mildenhall Air Base, Not brag, just fact. That's why the Office of Special Investigations or OSI used him for cases now and then.

His house was easily secured and a good place to work but as a living quarter it left something to be desired. A quick dinner of a Pork Pie and a bottle of Shandy he set to work.

Locking the door to his office, he opened the envelope and poured the contents onto a non-slip pad. A great many shreds poured out. Harry leaned back and blew out his cheeks, a good many hour's work was going to have to go into this one. This was going to be fun with a small "f".

What lay before him was like a jigsaw puzzle without a picture. The pieces were so similar they might have been identical. He reached for his magnifying head piece. It was similar to the one used by jewelers and he used it so he could work hands free. He rubbed his hands in satisfaction. He enjoyed a challenge, and this promised to be a big one. He had a photographic memory, a keen eye for details and plenty of patience. He was going to need all he possessed of the last one.

He chose the first piece and laid it on the pad, that was the easiest this was going to be. Now came the tedious part he had to sort through all the pieces to find the one that came either before or after the piece he had. Three hours later and he had three pieces he worked with covered tweezers and laid them on the disk so carefully they looked like one. As he assembled the pieces each one made the next one marginally easier.

"Yes!" he thought, "It was getting easier!" By two thirty he had completed the disk. "A place for everything and everything in its place" Harry thought happily. He picked up a high-powered magnifier as an adjunct to the one he was wearing. He had to check the entire disk to ensure everything was correct. This was a lot easier than putting it together so he could enjoy it. A few minor adjustments and the disk was ready to be sealed into a case for reading.

He suddenly realized how ravenous he was. What he needed was a full English fry up. In the kitchen he laid out all he needed for a feast. He picked up his fork and turned the sausages in the pan as they began to spit. These weren't the wieners he might get on base but Lincolnshire sausages not smoked and they had texture and taste. A couple of rashers of bacon, sliced tomatoes and mushrooms. He poured four beaten eggs into the pan; a giant omelet was in order. He licked his lips in anticipation and lit the gas under the baked beans. By the time he'd flipped his fry-up the beans would be ready.

Oliver knocked, entered, and stared. "Do you realize it's after 1600?" Harry swallowed and grinned. He tapped his plate with his knife. "I've just finished working so this is breakfast. Help yourself," he said nodding towards the teapot.

Oliver sipped his tea and leaned against the sink as Harry finished his repast. As Harry wiped his plate with a piece of bread he looked up and realized Oliver was showing signs of impatience. "I'm done so let's go into the lab. He let loose a maniacal laugh that set Oliver's hair on end. "Harry, I really wish you wouldn't do that. It gives me the creeps."

To the uninitiated Harry's computer was cumbersome and not recognizable as any model built. In truth he had made it himself from computers he'd bought and pieces he had had to order. It might not have been the most powerful, but it was capable of doing anything he needed from it.

Diagnostics and bootup took a while but once completed Harry placed the disk in the drive. The disk readout showed that it was holding more data than it should have been capable. "I'll feed it through a decompressor, and we'll be able to see what's on it." Once the disk was ready, he was about to enter the commands to read the files. Oliver interrupted him. "Sorry Harry, I'll have to do this without you watching." Harry smiled in resignation, "I thought you'd say that. I'll brew another cuppa." Oliver eventually came out holding seven disks including the original. "I deleted all the files and shut it down.

I know your dying to see what's on these but believe me you don't want to know."

Harry splashed his face and looked in the mirror, the sight wasn't impressive. A hot shower and shave and he felt much better. One thing he hadn't ever told Oliver about was the buffer drive, he booted it up and waited patiently.

It was like watching paint dry. Line by line a picture began to appear. Walls meeting at an angle – the corner of a room? A combo desk and shelves on the right. To the left a window and shades. Another couple of lines appeared revealing the desktop and the top of a building through the window – the room must be second story or third. Next the windowsill and what appeared to be a piece of cloth. The picture finished buffering and the rest burst upon the screen. Harry vomited. A bedroom. Below the window was a centered close up of a female face darkened from an infusion of blood. The eyes wild. The tongue swollen and stiff protruded from an open mouth. A thick cord cut into the neck making channels in the flesh. "Oh Christ, Oh Christ" he muttered, passing his arm over the cold sweat on his forehead. He put his head between his knees his breathing shallow.

Working to regain his composure he placed a piece of paper taped over the face and focused on the rest. With the horror gone he was able to concentrate on the window and desk. The desk type he associated with dorm rooms. The bed had the round knobs at the corners that was similar to dorm beds as well. He brought out a magnifying glass and his headpiece and looked at what was visible of the top of the building. A long band of white rectangle with a pole approximately 2 feet from the right side. A small black dent on the third panel and another dent in the second panel from the right was barely visible at the lower part of the window above the sill. He saved the picture and turned off the computer and headed into base.

Locking his car, he situated himself in front of the dorms and looked across the street at a long stretch of buildings. He walked from corner to corner, focusing on the details he had noted. It was near the end of the street when he saw the dark dent and the lighter one. He walked backwards across the street looking upwards to see if he could see a pipe extending from the roof. He tripped over the railing at the front of the dorm. He swiftly recovered and looked around hoping he hadn't been seen. Crossing the street back and standing under the dents, he took a pen out of his pocket and taking it apart screwed it back together as a scope. From his position he saw in reverse what had been seen in the photograph and identified the original location, second floor, corner room.

Mikey's Tea bar was just down the street. He called Oliver from a payphone outside. Oliver arrived in less than five minutes. He found Harry with a half-eaten burger and an almost empty Coke. "You must have a stomach like a garbage can!" Harry belched pleasurably as he finished off his meal. "Just felt a bit peckish so thought I'd top up while waiting" He passed over his notes. "I don't know how far you folks have gotten but I have located the room where the picture was taken." Oliver raised his eyebrows. "How the hell did you get the picture? I wiped everything!" Harry ignored the question and motioned for Oliver to follow "Come on, I'll show you." He pointed to a panel at roof height on a neighboring building. "Up there are the marks you can see from the window." He situated them centered from beneath the marks. "From here you can see that only one window is in position for seeing these marks as they are positioned in the pic.

Oliver nodded. "Gotcha" he said. The other windows view are being blocked from that pole. "Alright Sherlock, you might as well come with me." Oliver handed him a cloth mask and rubber gloves. They went to the dorm managers office and asked about the room in question. TSgt Lebolt got a key off a board and escorted them up the stairs. "This wing has been closed off for over a week due to a burst pipe. We moved everyone to another dorm or set them at the Bird in Hand Hotel just outside the gate. As they approached the room, the odor of decomposing human tissue was getting stronger with every step. Oliver waved the TSgt back, took the key and opened the door. The smell hit them all full in the face. The TSgt's face blanched and he excused himself outside as his face turned a pale green.

Oliver went inside holding his hand for Harry to remain where he was. He then did a cursory examination making notes. From a pack he had brought with him, he pulled out a camera and snapped a bunch of pictures from every angle and level. Over his shoulder he called in Harry. "Harry, you were right, look out the window from this angle and it's a match. Here is where he took the picture from." Harry entered the room to find Oliver kneeling at the corner of a bed. The remains on the bed was covered by a blanket. Harry walked outside and then back into the room flipping the blanket up to expose the shoes. "She was carried up and conscious when she was brought into the room. Her wrists were probably bound, or he had them clasped"

Oliver swung on him. "Go ahead, explain." Harry pointed towards the hall, "at the edge of the door she hooked her foot on the frame. There are scuff marks on the top of her shoe and there are corresponding marks on the edge of the door frame. Her hands were bound because she wasn't able to grab the other side."

Oliver looked at the frame and shoes, "alright so far, go on." Harry raised the blanket up to the neck. "She was picked up at probably the club or recreation center and they walked to either this room or someone's dorm room. She was either kicked out or left in a hurry. She was angry and must have been accosted most likely up the block."

Oliver sat down on the chair, "Ok, I'm still listening but I think I see your reasoning, the Club from the way she's dressed, The Rec center has a dance periodically so she might have been there with a group and separated to go with someone. So far I'm with you, but how do you know she was kicked out or left in a hurry?" "Her nylons are on inside out and are pretty twisted so she dressed in a hurry."

Harry closed his eyes to access his memory, "I walked the block before calling you. If you go up the sidewalk and follow from half the block suddenly, she is walking from the sidewalk onto the grass but parallel to the walk. You will see her heels in the dirt at an angle so you can see where she moved off the sidewalk. They go progressively further towards the curb which means someone was on the sidewalk and she was trying to avoid them."

A knock interrupted them. Oliver opened the door as the Mortuary team came in to take the remains to the Hospital. Oliver and Harry stood respectfully as the body was carried out. Once the remains were removed they locked the door sealing it with yellow tape, then returned the key and went outside.

Sitting in Mickey's Tea Bar at an isolated table by the back, they spoke softly. Oliver reached over for the sugar putting quite a bit in his tea. "Harry, with your eyes and the speed you can reason you really ought to cross train into investigations." Harry rubbed his temples, "We've been over this before, I can't take seeing certain things well, working mortuary and search and recovery is hard enough." Oliver nodded in understanding. "I know, but you handled upstairs alright." Harry took a drink of his tea. "I focused on the analysis and not on the corpus under the blanket, speaking of which we are looking for a pretty tall culprit with about a size 13 boot.

Oliver made a face when he drank his tea. He had distractedly added to much sugar. He ordered another cup and came back to the table. "Ok I get the height from where the door frame shoe marks were but how do you figure on the shoe size of the culprit." Harry grinned, "Come on you have that figured out just as easy as I did and it wasn't a shoe it was a boot. The lace around the neck was long enough to wrap around four times and still have enough to pull with so we know the boot was pretty large. We know it's a boot lace from the length, thickness and the cording in the material." Oliver headed to the door but asked Harry to stick around. To ensure Harry did he bought him a Fish and Chips lunch.

It didn't take long for Oliver to return and order lunch for himself. "Well, you have been cleared to work on the case with me, what do you say?" Harry grinned in spite of himself. "Ok partner you lead, and I'll follow." Oliver shook his head,

"Nope, you have been one step ahead already so for the moment let's say you're in charge."

Harry shrugged and added more vinegar to his fries. Oliver continued, "If we take it that she was starting from the Club or Rec center then the odds are she is either military or came with friends who were. There hasn't been a hue and cry about a missing person so I'm not sure where this leads us." Harry shook his head and started on more chips. "She may have been on leave just to hang out and see the sights or she just arrived and hasn't checked in with her squadron yet. If it's leave we'll know when her leave is up and she's a no show."

Oliver waited to see if Harry had finished, then he smugly leaned over the table and spoke softly. "Gottcha! When I was walking back I noticed on the sidewalk 6 cigs and the ashes were still fairly complete. The ashes were in large enough sections that it shows someone was taking long drags, from this I figure that person was waiting on her or someone to show. They were leaning against the wall most of the time but then walked to the corner a couple of times as if to check on something." Harry smote his forehead a blow and sat up. "Damn, your right I saw the butts but hadn't given them enough thought." Oliver's face was radiant, "I love it when I catch you out, it's so rare."

THE STORY SO FAR

Seated on a bench in the open air, they went over their progress so far. Oliver stretched and made himself more comfortable. He went over his notes out loud. "She was at the club or rec center. She was picked up by someone, who invited her up to their room. It was probably an officers quarters judging from the fact that it would have to be someone who had a room to themselves, airmen have to double up." Harry nodded in approval, Oliver continued, "She gets up to the room with them and does whatever she does if anything. We'll have to wait for the coroner's report to find out how far things went though. She may have got pissed, dressed quickly and left hurriedly as you suggest. She storms out to walk to somewhere when she is accosted by the other person. She tried to avoid them. They must have been talking to her since she didn't try to cross the street right away. Then they say something to upset her further, she turns to cross the street which would take her further away. That's when she's grabbed and carried into the room and is strangled to death."

Harry shuddered at the remembrance of the face he had seen. Being in Services should have given him time to get over his squeamishness with corpses completely. He was also on a Mortuary team and Search and Recovery and that should have helped as well. He already had dealt with a few mortuary cases and it was getting easier to handle being in their company, but it still was upsetting for him. It gave him nightmares after a case but if he shut down all emotions and focused on the job, he could get through it. Maybe that was what he'd always have to do.

They went into the club, Harry sat at a small table while Oliver interrogated the club barkeeper. It didn't take Oliver long to get the information he could. He informed Harry of what the conversation came to from his small notebook. "She came in alone, ordered a small sherry, Had one ring with a diamond and two diamond earrings. It was talked about as they didn't go with what she was wearing in their opinion and the diamond was an expensive one if real. She was approached by a tall man wearing just a shirt and black pants and combat boots. They didn't get a real good look at him as he was looking out over the crowd as he ordered, but he had short black hair. It was a slow night, only about twelve people there and most were regulars. Neither the girl nor guy were regulars, so they don't know much about them. Left together towards the end of the night. Oh, the guy kept trying to buy the girl drinks but she refused after the first one. Sounds to me like he wanted to get her drunk.

Harry's jaw clenched, he hated guys like that. He'd known a few in Services but had had a two-fisted conversation with them about it which seemed to change their minds or, if they continued had kept their mouth shut about it. Oliver suggested that the girl might have played tipsy out of curiosity regarding what he had in mind then when she found out, had read him the riot act and stormed out. Anyhow, they didn't have much of a description to go on. They finished off their drinks and headed outside to Harry's car.

Leaning against it they lit a couple of cigarettes and did some thinking. Harry took a deep drag, "When's the autopsy report due?" Oliver glanced at his watch, "Should be ready in an hour. Let's head into Mildenhall proper and grab a bite, we may not feel like it after we get the report." Harry slid behind the wheel and tried to start the car. Nothing but a short grind of the gears. With the resignation of long practice, he stepped outside and pushed, popping the clutch and dove in. The car roared into life and they sped off to the town of Mildenhall. Oliver piped up from the rear. "Just a thought, a starter isn't hard to put in, I'll even help if you want." Harry laughed, "I spend half my day on my ass. This gives me a little exercise although I usually park downhill just in case."

Oliver lay back and enjoyed the ride. As he sat there he closed his eyes and went over the case so far. Not much he had to admit but then, today was still the first day. Once they had the autopsy there might be some sort of a lead.

They pulled across from the Tea Shop and they went in to get something to eat. As Oliver ordered for both of them Harry played the two pence slot machine in the back. He gained ten pence and quit. Sitting down and waiting he was the various people come in and go. Most picked up lunch to go but a few sat and ate in the little seven table place. Over bangers chips and peas they ate without speaking.

Half an hour later Oliver looked at his watch. "We better get going." Harry ate the rest of his peas and got the car started. Driving onto Lakenheath Air base they pulled into the Hospital parking lot and headed for the coroner's office. Oliver got Harry passed through and they walked down the long hallway in the basement. The Coroner was a small man barely five feet, maybe just a little over. He had a bald pate and thick glasses. He was very methodical and deliberate in his actions. It took a while before the Coroner was ready.

"Well, we have a few things for you. She was throttled as is shown by the occlusion in the face and the deep indentations from the laces. She was drugged or at least an attempt was made to drug her for we found traces of Parafon 40, a muscle relaxant, in her system. Not a full dose but enough to slow her down. From the marks on her wrists she was held down and an attempt was made to penetrate however full penetration was not achieved. There is skin under her fingernails we are attempting to get more information on. There is strain on the feet as if she had attempted to hold onto something with half the tops of her feet. She was approximately 23 and weighed 110 lbs. There was alcohol in her blood but not much, about .02. I may have more for you tomorrow but that's all that I have, other then what we discussed earlier. "Thanks Sir," Oliver and Harry shook hands with the Coroner and walked back to the car.

"I think she must have realized he tried to drug her. That's when she booked out of there." Oliver agreed. "Let's get back to our base and look around I want to see which dorms are closest to there.

As he drove Harry opened his mind to Oliver. "I want you to do something. The picture I saw was done by someone who knows how to take pictures. See if you can arrange a Photography contest or something. If we go over the pictures of the applicants, we might be able to figure out something from the other pictures. An avid photographer will jump at any chance to show off and there was something artistic in the way that picture was taken." Oliver closed his eyes to imagine the photograph again. "You may have something. Good focus on the foreground, the main emphasis centered and clear, he had to position himself to take the picture so it was something he wanted to be done special. Yeah artistic is a good way to put it. He could have just snapped a pic if he wanted to record the body but it was framed so to speak." Harry took up the conversation again, "It takes talent to take a picture like that because you have to know how to adjust for focus and focal plane. That means a full operational camera, so we aren't looking for someone with a Kodak Instamatic. Looks more like a professional's camera, plus the fact that they have a scanner shows they have money to spend too, those things aren't cheap.

Oscar folded his arms and his head dropped as he thought deeply. "I'll get something going, I may see about doing it in the base Library. We'll wangle some sort of prize and get as wide a sampling as we can. I want you to take another look at the rest of the pictures on the disk and mark down any abnormalities to look for, either that or any identifying characteristics." Harry dropped Oscar off and then went home. He had a lot of work to do.

After three days of concentrated effort, Harry had a list that should help if this plan worked. All the pictures had a minute triangle at the right top corner, a minor defect in the lens not readily viewable but clear when looked at closely. The photographer had a mania for large close center focus but they framed it with things on either side. The film was all high speed indicated by the clarity. The photographer generally used an umbrella light as the light source was mostly the same. There were several other points, but these should be enough to narrow down the field.

Word went out that there was to be a Photography exhibition and contest at the base Library. All comers welcome, first prize was fifty pounds. Harry and Oliver were looking at the flyers. Some were in base shop windows, some on posts and some on at the Tea Bar. At Harry's request several were around the Taxi stand. Oliver was using his connections to have some of the security forces in plain clothes on hand as well.

LIGHTS, CAMERA, ACTION

The day before the event Oliver and Harry as well as several of the Security Police had gone through every entrant with Harry's notes on what to look for in front of them. These had narrowed the field to two people. One was listed as a mechanic Staff Sergeant and the other as a first lieutenant from Base Operations. While people were coming in to view the pictures on display Harry wandered around looking at the entrants seated watching.

Harry spotted the Lt and sat down next to him. "I was looking at your pictures, you have a very distinct style, what kind of camera do you use." The lieutenant peered intently into Harry's friendly face, "Its a Cannon F1 but I don't use the auto settings, what's yours." Harry hung his head, "I usually use an Argus, but I do have a Rolleiflex for when I want to take a little better pic." The lieutenant perked up, "I'd like to see the Rolleiflex, they're pretty rare usually, not many people still have em." Harry grinned, "I can bring it up to show you sometime, where do you hang out? I love looking at photography stuff. My dad used to work for a photo lab and the smell of developer is like perfume to me." The Lt laughed, "Yeah me too, I even have an enlarger! Have you ever seen a scanner?" Harry got a puzzled look on his face, "I've heard about them but they're hella expensive." Bring your camera's up and you can see my equipment. In fact, why don't you come up now. He pulled on Harry's arm, jerking him out of his seat and placing an arm firmly around his shoulder drew him outside. Harry saw the flash of a knife blade hidden in his palm but close to his throat.

He tried to catch Oliver's eye as they passed around the back of the judges table, but Oliver was looking front and center. He really should have told Oliver he was going to walk around before he did, now it was too late. Outside they walked towards the officer quarters. It was dark, the Lieutenant had Harry's arms pinned behind him with one hand and kept the other clasped on the back of his neck squeezing tightly. Harry became disoriented from the pressure and he stumbled as he was forced forward.

TROUBLE FOR HARRY

Harry knew he had little chance of escaping, though smart in many ways the finer points of fight and flight were not in his forte.

Once at the officer's dorm He let one of Harry's arms go for a moment but chopped Harry efficiently on the back of his neck. Harry was carried to the first door on the right. When his head cleared he was strapped into a chair. A bright light hurt his eyes. He focused on a camera that was sitting on a table nearby. The Lieutenant leaned over facing Harry. "You were curious about my equipment. He stroked the camera lovingly. This is my record keeper. I only use it for special pictures. You will make an alright study. You aren't my preferred type of subject but I guess you'll do." He went around to the back of the chair.

A strap was placed around Harry's throat and tightly secured. Harry could barely breathe. "My names Frank by the way, not that you'll remember it." he grinned as he picked up the camera. "look up a little more." Harry's breath was thin and his throat was beginning to swell constricting him even more. Frank squatted down to get a better picture. Changing lenses, he held up Harry's face into the light. "Good, the colors coming up and your eyes are beginning to bulge."

Harry tried to look towards the door. Frank noticed the slight cast of his eyes. "Are you hoping for rescue my friend? Tut tut, I added a few more bolts to the door. I'm afraid that even if they should get in it will take them too long to do so. He sat opposite Harry with the Camera on his lap. "I wasn't expecting to take pictures or I would have gotten more film today. No matter, we'll wait till you are further along before we take more. You're holding on better than most my friend.

Harry's eyes were watering, and he could barely keep them open. He was distinctly lightheaded. His swollen tongue was beginning to protrude. Frank took another picture. Through the blur before his eyes he saw a slight movement at the window. For just a moment he thought the light from outside was blanked out. Suddenly the window shattered. Oliver and the Security team burst through. The security police tackled Frank and Oliver loosened the belt on Harry's neck undoing the straps as fast as possible. As security read Frank his rights and led him outside Oliver helped Harry as best he could. Looking outside the broken window he saw with relief the ambulance and the OSI team. Harry was carried out to the ambulance as the OSI sealed off the room and started taking evidence and statements.

In the Hospital at Lakenheath, Harry spent part of his leave time getting himself back in order. His throat was still sore, and he had a massive headache. That cleared up when Oliver showed up with a Security Forces person. "Hey buddy, how about doing some work instead of lolling around." Harry's voice came out in a hoarse croak. "What do you have in mind?" Out of the box Oliver pulled a 386 laptop and a few external disks. Apparently, Frank had done a lot of compressing of files and partitioning disks to make them harder to read. Harry asked Oliver to get his toolkit from his car and bring it to him. He had a few disks that should be able to crack this stuff open in no time. Oliver left giving instructions to the SP, no one was allowed in until he got back. The SP apparently took his job very seriously because Harry didn't get lunch.

Oliver arrived in record time. He handed over the kit and sat down to order them both something to eat. Harry worked away even as his meal came and got cold. Once Harry had loaded up his command program he was able to unlock all the files quickly. What showed up he didn't look at but handed the packs and laptop to Oliver. "Let me know what you find." he croaked. Oliver waved and went out but he made sure Harry would get his meals.

Three days later Harry was home and feeling better. Oliver showed up and the two chatted for a while. "O.k." Oliver fished out his notebook and began. "The girl was Amn, Loren Dune just arrived from Cleveland. She was brought to the dance at the club by a couple of girls who had met her at the rec center. She was doing her in processing and wasn't expected until yesterday. When she didn't show, security was called to check on her. The description of the Airman they were expecting and our corpus matched. We passed on the other pictures to the Police in town to see if they could identify the other seven since nobody else on base has come up missing."

Harry nodded, "How did you locate me?" Oliver lay back in his chair grinning. "You left a great trail. It's a good thing you put a lot of polish on your shoes. I found the three marks you made going to the door, then just followed whenever you had stumbled and made another one. They stopped about where the Officer Dorms were but his umbrella light was so bright it must have bounced off a picture glass and was visible in the crack of the curtain. The rest you know. Harry shook his head. "I tried to do an OSI's job and darn near got killed being smart."

Oliver lent forward and peered into his friend's face. "Once you get a little training under your belt, you'll do a lot better." Harry half rose from his seat. "What are you talking about?" Oliver handed him an envelope. Out slid a temporary badge with his name on it. "You'll have to go for training but we have arranged for you to come back here and you'll be working with me." Harry shook his head unbelieving. "What about the computer systems. They don't know how to keep them running."

Oliver refilled his tea and settled more comfortably in his chair. "I saw your logbooks, it's all there and if they're smart they'll find someone as conscientious as you were. Thirteen books of every problem and procedure is pretty impressive.

Let's get you packed. I'll drive you to the airport. You'll have to go to Randolph in Texas for your initial training. Before we go though, let's clean *all* your hard drive.

MYSTERY IN A TEACUP

Harry was sitting in the small tea shop in Mildenhall with a pot of tea and a plate of scones sitting in front of him. it was to be an aperitif to the full breakfast he had ordered. This had become a regular routine now as often as he could. The owner brought plate after plate and set them before him. Harry dug in with gusto, A full British breakfast set him up for the day and he looked forward to it. The manager sat down at Harry's table and chatted a while. Harry had quickly learned that if he came into places and kept his mouth shut people would join him and talk to him. It was his way of meeting people. He wasn't sure what it was, but people automatically took him for an American. The fact that he was a quiet American was enough for the locals to find him intriguing. Harry liked the little restaurant and brought his friends with him often. The owner Matty welcomed them with graciousness and a warm smile. He always felt like an honored guest.

Today Matty wasn't smiling though, in fact, she seemed nervous and after fidgeting with the plates and cups for a while she finally opened her mind to Harry. "Do you mind if I talk to you for a bit?" Harry pushed aside his empty plates and poured them both a cup of tea. He turned as receptive a face to Matty as he could and waited for more. "Someone has been trying to damage my business. I've had orders canceled and my drains were plugged up yesterday. They found a rag blocking the pipes. Two days ago, an order of flour and sugar was delivered to my back door. I was taking care of a few customers and by the time I got out back to bring it in all the bags were slashed. I salvaged what I could, but it still shorted me a lot. I can't imagine who would be out to ruin me. There aren't a lot of places here and I don't have anyone who hates me that much that I know of." To her surprise Harry jumped up and ran out to a phone box. He came in five minutes later rubbing his hands and grinning.

"Matty, I am now on leave for a few days. With your permission I am going to work here for the time being. Maybe together we can solve your problem." She clasped his hand with tears rolling down her cheeks. Harry held her hands for a moment then brought out a notebook. "If I'm going to be of any help there are a few questions I have to ask." She wiped her eyes and sat up straight ready to answer. "O.k. first off, are there any new restaurants opening nearby that might want you out of the way?" Matty gave a negative nod of the head. "Second, have you had to let anyone go recently?" Again, the negative inclination, she had always run it alone. "Hmm, you say that you don't have anyone that doesn't like you, but have you had any angry customers recently?" Again, a negative response.

Harry scratched his head and leaned back in his chair. There just didn't seem to be any reason for anyone trying to hurt her or her business. As they sat discussing her problem her two children came in. They helped themselves to some tea and sausage rolls and sat down at the table with Harry and Matty. They accepted Harry as a friend and would show him their homework and tell him about their day. Mary was 12 and Thomas was 9. They finished up their homework as they munched away on the rolls.

Harry looked at their notebooks as they worked. Thomas's was very straightforward, and his pages were free of embellishments. Mary's pages though were covered in artwork.

Anything she didn't have to turn in was covered in pictures from stick figures climbing up the edge of the lines to animals walking around the margins. As she turned the pages, he saw pictures she had drawn of her friends. She was quite a proficient artist. Mary looked at the clock and then shoved her books in her bag, gulped the last of her tea and grabbed her brother both of them hurtling out the door and down the street. Matty cleared the table as Harry worked out how to help.

He had a look out the back of the place and decided that with a camera set to take pictures every five minutes or so he might be able to see if anyone was sneaking around. He pulled out his Bolex super 8 camera and set it. He placed it on the window ledge looking outside so that it could see the drain and anything by the back door. He cleaned a spot on the window so the pictures would be clearer. Next thing he knew he was cleaning all the windows back and front. Matty laughed when she saw him working diligently at a corner getting some gum off. As the camera clicked Harry went about the daily routine of the Tea Shop. Taking orders and helping in the kitchen sweeping and generally, keeping things going. Matty's order was dropped off at the back door. Harry waited a bit to see if anything would happen. He heard running feet and quickly opened the door. Whoever it was, was incredibly fast. A neat slash was directly across the bags at about 3 feet high. Harry examined the cuts and took pictures with his Argus before taking the bags inside, taping them and placing them on the shelves. Figuring that he had what he wanted he took down the Bolex and had the film developed. Tomorrow they would have a picture of the culprit.

Harry was at the Tea Shop early and helped setting up. He made a batch of Scotch Eggs and meat pasties. When he had cleaned up he ran to the photo lab and picked up his film. From the boot of his car he got out a video editor. The small screen would let him check out what they had captured without having to drag out a movie projector and screen. Seated at the corner table he flipped the editors light switch and started cranking. He worked his way through speeding up as fast as he was able until he found the spot he wanted from yesterday. "Just great!" he muttered as he saw that all he had caught was the back of a red jacket with a leopard head on it. He did a sketch of the leopard and filed it into his notebook. Not much to go on but sometimes the smallest clue can bust the doors wide open.

He packed up the equipment and put it all in the back of the trunk. Walking in he saw Mary and Thomas bent over their books. It was Saturday but they wanted to get their homework over with so they could have the day for playing. Matty brought over a pot of tea and a couple of cups for herself and Harry along with some of the Scotch Eggs. As they ate Mary saw that Harry was admiring some of her drawings.

"You really have talent and a great sense of humor." She passed her notebook to him and allowed him to flip through the pages. He saw various pictures of animal's birds, landscapes and even a picture of her school. On the side of the doorway, she had drawn a picture of a Leopard. "Is that your schools' mascot?" he asked her. In answer she opened one of her books to show a sticker emblazoned on the cover. Harry pulled out his sketch and was surprised to see that they matched. Mary laughed when she saw his drawing. True, it wasn't a good likeness and more of a caricature of the logo but the similarities were evident. It looked to Harry as if it might be someone from the school.

He flipped through the pictures that Mary had drawn of her friends. He noticed that one of the pictures had an X crossing it. "Mary, why the X over this guy?" Mary glanced over and then turned back to her work. "He's a idiot. He used to be my friend or at least I thought he was. I heard him talking about me when he didn't know I was there. He used to come here a lot and I'd treat him to something to eat or drink. He didn't like me after all, he just wanted free food."

Harry was sympathetic. It hurts when people use you. Harry now had a good idea of what was happening. This was a case of payback for him being deprived of free food. Now the question was how to handle it. It was time to bring Matty up to date. "I'm not surprised it's him if it is. Something about him makes me nervous and I never liked him hanging around. He used to come back behind the counter and take things as if he owned the place. I didn't say anything for Mary's sake."

Harry decided to talk to the local constabulary. He invited him to the Tea Shop and filled him with a large breakfast, then showed him his evidence. "Sir, I'm not sure what our options are. I think we know who and why but now the question becomes what to do about it. Constable Jarvis leaned back and picked his teeth. "I'm glad you brought this to my attention. I'd like you to do me a favor and leave it with me. When's your next shipment of supplies. Harry checked his notes and pointed out that a small order of eggs and sugar was to be delivered today. "Should be here about 1300, sorry one o'clock." Constable Jarvis decided he'd stick around then since it was already after noon. It was a quiet morning and he invited Harry to go for a little walk with him. They didn't walk far but meandered around the Market stalls watching the people milling about and buying from the various sellers. A small truck emerged from the alley behind where the Tea Shop was located. Constable Jarvis pulled Harry by the arm. He cautiously peered around the corner. Your inventory has arrived. I'm sorry but in order to catch our friend in the act I am going to let him slice your stock. It's usually in a straight line so it won't spoil it all and we'll have the evidence to show malicious intent and destruction of property.

Constable Jarvis lit a cigarette and leaned against the wall peering down the alley. He was just out of sight but had a clear view. Harry standing behind him saw him stiffen in readiness. The sound of running feet, the smooth sound of a knife tearing through paper and then the louder sound of the feet reaching the street. Constable Jarvis stepped backwards and stretched out his arm. As a head and shoulders emerged from the alley, he swiftly grabbed at a coat collar jerking the person backwards and then held the young man by the front of the coat. "Your nicked old son." The face that was presented to Harry went through a variety of emotions, first was triumphant elation then shock followed by anger, resignation and last fear as he looked into Constable Jarvis's face.

"Son, I think you owe some people an apology." The constable growled as he dragged the miscreant to the door of the tea shop and pushed him through. Matty whipped around as she heard his screech and flop on the tiled floor. The young man apologized but without seeming to mean it. "Well john, I guess it's time to head to the station." That seemed to get his attention. He snapped around and faced his father. "Pop, you can't mean it! You wouldn't put me in quad!" Constable Jarvis's face crumbled. "Son, you haven't left me any other option. I've covered for you many times and now you seem to think the rules don't apply to you, well guess what, they apply to you and me the same as for anyone else." He turned to Matty. "Ma'am, I'm going to have to ask you to come with me and file charges." Matty turned to Harry, "can you hold down the shop for a bit Harry, this shouldn't take long." She grabbed a sweater and accompanied Jarvis and John out the door. As they walked out onto the street Jarvis placed the handcuffs onto his wailing son and led the way to the station.

Harry made the kids lunch and helped customers all the time wondering if Matty would really press charges. Harry was surprised after two hours passed and Matty had not returned. Evening was approaching and Matty returned all smiles and almost giddy. Harry brewed them a pot and sat down for the explanation. "Thank you, Harry, were not going to have any problems anymore." She sipped at her steaming cup. "PC Jarvis placed his son into a cell and let him simmer there for a few hours. By the time we had had a chat and gotten to know each other he decided it might be a good Idea to check on his son. John was curled up in a ball on the bare mattress still crying. I declined to press charges and he promised we wouldn't have any more problems with him. In fact he is going to pay back for what he damaged." She lay back in her chair. "It's a shame you can't stay on here Harry, it's been a lot easier on me lately."

Harry wiped the table and removed his apron. As he went out the door he turned with a smug grin, "have fun on your date with Jarvis tonight!" Her cup fell onto the table as she looked herself over. How the hell did he know?

MURDER IN THE MORNING

Camping should be done properly in wide open spaces and with miles of areas to walk in and explore especially with a dog. Yet here Harry was on the back of the base doing what he considered processed camping. He had a couple of days off but was on call, so the Family camp site at the back of the base was the best he could do. At least it had a lake and small wooded area. Harry had gone off duty last night and sped immediately to the family camp to make the most of his off time. He had pitched his tent and sat up watching the full moons rise reflected in shimmering ripples off the lake the sound of birds lulling him to sleep. After OSI Tech school and his first few cases this was the first real day off in a year and a half. He slept soundly waking early to fish for his breakfast.

A couple of fresh catfish for breakfast with a pot of coffee was a sufficient start for the day. His dog Juno had caught his own fish and Harry had dutifully cooked it for him as well. He walked the half mile to the showers, changed then most importantly, clipped the beeper to his side and checked his blackberry. Inhaling the fresh air scented with pine and fish water he set his feet towards a trail he hadn't explored yet.

The path was narrow and showed limited usage which suited him just fine. As he walked he was aware of the life surrounding him. He could read the presence of animals through subtle signs. The footprints, a small patch of fur, patches of bare spaces on trees all told a story of the animals surrounding him. As he surveyed the ground he saw only one other set of human footprints. Male he thought, must have been rather heavyset since the footprints were deep. Tall considering the stride I'd say about 5'9" or thereabouts he mused. Slightly off balanced since one foot was deeper than the other. His blood ran cold for a moment as he pictured this person in his mind. Not off balance, more probable he was carrying someone or something on his shoulder. He followed the footprints along as they veered off the path for a dense wooded area. Juno wandered over the slightly damp track, exploring for a moment then rushing off to explore other scents. With a sense of foreboding he walked to the center of the area where the footprints led, A fresh and large log was laid recently with several smaller lying around. Many older logs had been placed here and the birds used them for bugs and grubs that burrowed inside.

Probably just one of the rangers laying out new logs to decompose and feed the critters he thought. "Come on Juno" He called as Juno was busy nosing at one of the stacks of logs. Juno started barking and digging. Harry rushed over to see what Juno was trying to get at. Juno began to whine as he dug away. Harry helped Juno to uncover whatever he had smelt. Slowly Harry dismantled the stack of wood. Half way down he came upon a small patch of corduroy visible at the bottom. He worked harder to uncover the patch in full and with Juno's help they got down to expose the whole. An old couch cover was exposed along with several tennis balls. Juno barked and leapt about grabbing a ball and running around with it. Harry grabbed another ball and as they walked further down the path he threw them for Juno to chase and return.

An hour later the path veered off to the right and paralleled the lake for a while. Harry took a break and sat on a stump.

Juno dropped a ball at Harry's feet which he promptly threw in the water. Juno bound in and swam out to bring it back. Juno finally tired out and laid down beside Harry. From where Harry was sitting he could see out over the lake back to his camp site. He followed the course of the lake from the right scanning the bank and chewing on a piece of grass. To his right at about twenty yards was another small beach area. On the bank he could see trash that had washed up. A red cooler, cans of beer, and something long colored red, blue, and red again. He brought out his binoculars and tried to get a better look. Enlarged now he distinguished the child's clothing. The arms bent under a red capped head, a blue shirt and red pants. Small tennis shoes were on the feet. "Come on Juno" he called to his dog, "I don't like the look of this." He waded out into the lake and walked to the beach. The going was slow as his feet were sucked into the sandy lake bottom but he struggled through and made the shore eventually. Juno who had swam all the way was barking and jumping to welcome him.

Harry approached the small form lying in the sand. He kneeled down beside it and turned it over. The face that was revealed was blank. Softly Harry cursed. It was one of those dolls people put up that look like a kid playing hide and seek. He took it apart cursing all the while and placed the remnants in a plastic bag he located on the shore. Tying the bag up he placed it near the cooler then went in search of the path again.

It took about ten minutes of walking but they ended back at the first clearing they had stopped at. Harry decided to go back to camp and have some lunch. Heating up a Meal Ready to Eat ration he settled down to enjoy as best he could his packet of Tuna Casserole. He reached into the plastic pack and pulled out cheese and crackers. He spread the processed jalapeño cheese onto the crackers and munched those down sharing them with Juno. Juno took one bite and spit it out. Resting, Harry laughed at the events of the morning. His overactive imagination had been working hard all the time seeing possible crime scenes where none existed. He placed Juno's leash on him and tied him off so he wouldn't run away then lay down for a nap.

Waking up refreshed by his short nap Harry decided another walk was in order. Untying Juno he found another side trail that went deep into the center of the forested area. He brought a flashlight with him in case the walk was longer than he anticipated. This time Juno was content to walk along side Harry. Slowly evening came on and the full moon rose giving light to the path around him. Harry looked up and then stiffened in his tracks. Ahead and to the right he saw a person dangling from a tree. Arms and legs fell loosely at its side a rope attached to the branch above. He reached for his blackberry to put in a call to Oliver. "Better make sure before I do, the way today has been going who knows." He informed Juno who was seated next to him waiting patiently. In the shadowy light of the moon it certainly looked like a hanged person. He tried to use his flashlight but the light wasn't enough to illuminate from this distance. As they approached the tree where the supposed body was Juno started whining. "You think something's wrong to don't you boy." Suddenly with a bark Juno bounded forward towards the tree stretching to his full length up the trunk barking continually. Harry ran to join Juno. Just as he approached he turned his flashlight onto the tree. He was next to Juno when he saw it. A skunk was treed just out of Juno's reach. He tried to pull Juno away but he was too late, both were skunked. He flashed his light up the trunk to the branch where he had seen the silhouette. The sight that met his eyes made him sit down on the ground and shake himself. The body was a broken branch dangling from a long swath of bark from the end of the rest of the branch.

"Come on Juno, it's going to take a while to get us cleaned up." Several baths and several hours later they were tolerably clean enough to go to sleep. In the morning Harry packed up and dropped Juno off at home. Another shower and he went into work. Oliver looked up from the reports he was reading. "Glad your back we have a new case to work on. Seems a body was found in a dumpster behind the base exchange." He was a little surprised at Harry's enthusiasm until Harry described his relaxing camping trip. Laughing Oliver closed the file and locked up his paperwork. "Come on Harry let's get to work on a real case." Both laughing, they headed out the door and went to work.

MURDER IN MUCK

Agents Oliver and Harry approached the Commissary. Due to something that was found out back it was prematurely closed. Customers were making their way to their cars and a security forces airman was guiding them out of the parking lot. The uniformed guards as well as cones and barricades hastily placed in front effectively held back the crowd of curious onlookers. Walking past the flashing lights of the patrol cars they were met by SSgt Paxton of Security Forces. His team was already on the job taking pictures and doing a check of the area. SSgt Paxton led them to the rear of the Commissary filling them in as he escorted them. "Looks like someone bashed this poor guy over the head with something large and flat, probably something like a wide bladed shovel. From the way the body is positioned he was dumped soon after the attack. The evening shift was dumping trash when they found the body."

Oliver and Harry could hear the soft buzz of many flies as they approached the dumpster. The flies rose in a cloud as Harry peered in. He brought out his camera and began snapping his own pictures of the corpse, the dumpster and the surrounding area. SSgt Paxton checked with Oliver and Harry to ensure they had seen everything they needed to. "O.k. let's get the body out." As a team in white coveralls carefully extradited the remains from the can Harry noticed that the rigor was still present enough that the body came out mostly stiff in its current position. The head was bent sideways, the legs bent backwards, arms splayed and out at the sides. No attempt was made to hide the body. "We'll take him to the morgue, come on down in about an hour and we'll give you a preliminary report, alright?"

Harry and Oliver conducted an intensive survey noting the clutter surrounding the dumpster, Empty produce boxes littered the side, but were not broken down and placed in the dumpster or recycling bin. There were grease trails leaking out of a rusted hole in the side of the dumpster mixed with the tar that had leaked out of a few barrels carelessly laid on their sides. There was a ladder on the right side of the door that had patches of grease stains which had to make climbing it hazardous. On the ground wilted lettuce was strewn around as though birds had been enjoying the feast left out for them.

Harry took plenty of more snaps from every angle, even lying on the ground for some all the while Oliver was making notes and measuring positions of everything. Harry went and put his film into the OSI lab with a rush order on them. As they waited they went back over the crime scene again by themselves. Oliver stood in the middle of the back lot and looked at the ground, up to the roofs, at the gate etc. "You know Harry. I've got an odd feeling about this. Something doesn't feel right." Harry shrugged his shoulders, "Let's wait for the report before we jump to any conclusions but I have to say I'm inclined to agree with you." Harry did a walk around but couldn't see anything more than they had already noticed. They walked to the morgue to see if they could gain any new information.

The mortuary office was pretty barren except for the large open area that was used for visiting next of kin. The area where MSgt Powell had his office was fairly empty except for a metal desk, a book case of regulations, a locking file cabinet and a small television tray that held a coffee pot, sugar and creamer. As they waited for the report they sipped at oily and gritty coffee. Oliver topped up his cup with as much sugar and creamer as he discreetly could. Captain Baker, the Mortuary Officer came in with his findings and handed them to Powell. MSgt Powell stood as the captain walked in, "Thanks Sir, care for a cup of coffee?" The captain beat a hasty retreat. Apparently he had had Powell's coffee before.

MSgt Powell glanced over the paper before opening his mind to Harry and Oliver. "Well, not much to go on. His clothes are clean except for some garbage on his shirt and pants, grease, eggs, bananas etc.. He didn't have a wallet or identification on him so we're sending a picture around to the First Sergeants to identify. We should hear something by tomorrow morning. It looks like he died without any struggle sometime about 0800. On his shoes is a small amount of black grease or tar that looks pretty recent. His head was cracked so the strike came with excessive force. Harry contemplated that phrase, was their some kind of acceptable force? Once we hear back from the squadrons we may have more to go on.

Back at their office they went over the pictures of the crime scene. Working with magnifying glasses they tried to work out anything they might have missed while doing an eyes on the ground. The area was not exactly conducive to the tracing of foot marks and tell tale cigarette butts. Cigarettes were plentiful by the door since it was the natural place for a quick smoke without the boss seeing. Towards evening they were no further forward and decided to wait till tomorrow for anything security may turn up.

Harry was getting used to the fact that working for OSI was not as exciting as he thought it might be. It was all about details and putting pieces of information together. He still shuddered when he thought about the first case he worked on. It damn near got him killed. A breath of air seemed to be in order. Walking around the base was a pleasant evening activity. Tonight, his steps led him to the club. He spent the evening walking through it and listening in on conversations. He was fairly nondescript looking and could wander around without drawing attention. Sometimes he picked up a few pieces of information this way. Tonight though, he wasn't lucky. Nobody was talking about anyone missing. His beeper went off just as he was thinking about going home. Softly cursing under his breath, he saw that Oliver wanted to meet up, the body had been identified.

The Services First Sergeant was MSgt Thomas. She was seated behind the desk with a file folder in front of her looking distraught. "I don't understand who would do this, especially to Airman West. He was pretty quiet, did his job and went home. He worked in the flight kitchen by himself. Everybody seemed to like him and from what I know he didn't have any enemies." She reached into a locked cabinet and pulled out a key with a tag on it. It was balanced in the palm of her hand and she looked at it thoughtfully. "I've got the key to his dorm room so we might as well get this over with." With a deep sigh she led the way to the dorms. The cool evening made the three blocks walk almost enjoyable. They entered a long brick building climbing to the fourth floor and then to the third door on the right.

In Amn West's room Oliver and Harry were surprised by how barren it was. The bed was neatly made complete with hospital corners. On the shelf in the desk/bookcase stood five study guides containing all the rules and regulations to all aspects of Services functions. The only other objects were a collection of joke books, a few gags such as the kind you would find in a joke shop and a magic 8 ball. His clothes were folded neatly in the drawer and his pressed uniforms were hanging orderly in the closet.

"How long had he been here?" Harry asked as he looked around the spartan room. His immediate thoughts were that the airman must have only recently arrived. MSgt Thomas leaned back against the bookcase. "About three and a half years. He signed up for four and was planning on getting out at the end of his term. We were his first base." Oliver straightened up from looking under the bed. "It really doesn't look like he did much besides go to work and come home. Do you know if he hung out with anyone?" MSgt Thomas shook her head. "He was always ready to help out wherever and whenever it was needed but didn't seem to have much of a life outside work. His supervisor is coming over, in fact she should be here already." A knock on the door and SSgt Susan Merry walked in. From the look in her eyes it was apparent she was taking the death of an airman under her authority hard.

She didn't have a lot of information to offer. He was a good worker who was able to run the Flight Kitchen on his own after only a week of training. He was a bit of a prankster but that was all. She smiled as the thought of some of his pranks came to mind. "He liked to have a good time with people. Once he put my Scooter in the freezer. It was on the back dock but when

I went to look for it, it was gone. It took me twenty minutes before I found it. I wasn't mad because it roared into life when I started it. He played pranks on everybody but it was all in fun and nobody ever got mad. Everybody plays a few pranks on everybody else. It keeps the strain of a long day from getting to them."

Oliver folded his arms and leaned back against the wall. "Seems like a guy who's gonna be missed. Some people have a natural way of knowing how to make the workday better. Are you sure that he didn't get anyone upset with his tricks?" SSgt Merry shook her head vigorously. "No chance, If he had, whoever was upset would have been in my office like a shot. Things going bad get reported right away and dealt with just as fast." Harry nodded in acknowledgement. He still kept in touch with some of the people in Services and West's name came up frequently. He was usually mentioned with a grin and his latest exploits would be repeated with smiles all round. He just hadn't ever met the guy. Oliver pushed himself off the wall, "We'll have a talk to the folks at the dining facility and see where that leads us. I'll take the night shift and you Harry, get the dayshift." Harry grimaced. He knew that the night shift would only have a couple of people to interview whereas dayshift had about eighteen!

Harry arrived at the Dining Hall just before the breakfast hours ended. He walked in line with a few stragglers who had also come in as the meal was set to close. He ordered a cheese omelet and biscuits with gravy then sat down at the back of the dining hall. SSgt Merry sat down with him and offered the use of her office for the interviews. Harry accepted. The interviews took most of the day as Oliver knew that they would, that was why he had taken the night shift. He had finished in half an hour. Harry asked his questions sympathetically. He commiserated with them on the loss of their comrade and then launched into his questions. All the stories were pretty much the same. West was a great guy to work with, a fun guy who played pranks or made people laugh with jokes. Everyone was broken up about his death and it seemed as if the heart had been taken out of it. As Harry walked around it seemed the heart of the place really was gone. People were doing their job but there was little joy in anyone's face.

Harry walked out the back door and headed over to Micky's Tea Bar. With a cup of tea and four hamburgers he began to feel a little better. He was finishing his third when Oliver showed up. He grabbed some fish and chips and sat down at Harry's table. "Seems like we're not getting anywhere are we?" Oliver proclaimed as he doused his lunch in malt vinegar. Harry coughed as the pungent fumes assailed his nostrils. "You're going to burn out your innards using so much!" Oliver dipped his already sodden fish into the juice at the bottom and pushed the whole piece into his mouth. Swallowing the piece he quickly readied the next one. "Harry, I swear something about this tells me we're on the wrong track. Unless there is a lunatic roaming the base, which I doubt, I can't see any reason why someone would have clubbed this guy. Everything I know tells me something is missing." Harry quickly finished off the last part of the hamburger and brushed the crumbs from his shirt and pants. "Hurry up and eat then let's take another look. I've got a feeling your right. Oliver dunked the last of his fish and popped it into his mouth. There must have been an overabundance of vinager because he went into a prolonged coughing spell while Harry helped him as best he could laughing all the while.

As they walked, Oliver and Harry reviewed in their heads the interviews and all they had studied from the pictures. Arriving at the back of the Commissary, Oliver walked around while Harry sat against the wall accomplishing a mental inventory of his surroundings. The dumpster was centered on the wall with the double door to the right of it. Beside the door was a pile of egg cartons with expired eggs. The dumpster was full of rotten lettuce, oranges and moldy potatoes. Oliver was looking carefully in the dirt surrounding the dumpster without finding anything. He came over to Harry and sat beside him. "Hey, were on duty, you can't fall asleep on the job."

Harry opened his eyes and a gentle smile crossed his lips. His eyes had that dreamy quality of someone remembering a fond memory. "I was just going back in time about 18 years. The eggs reminded me of it." Oliver took out a cigarette and handed one to Harry. "Wanna tell me about it?" Harry snickered as he lit the Winston. "I was thinking about the time my older sister's boyfriend took me out for the day. I was about nine I think and he and I went to the corner store. He bought us sodas and then we went to the back of the store. Outside there were a few cartons of rotten eggs. He had me stuff as many as I could into my shirt and then we climbed onto the roof. From the street you never would have seen us. We'd keep a careful eye out and when someone came by we'd toss an egg down at them. We bombed about twenty people before the manager caught us. As he came up the ladder we shinnied down the drain pipe and beat it for home. We could still hear him cursing us out as we rounded the corner." Oliver took a deep drag. "Quite the prankster weren't you." At the word prankster Harry and Oliver both glanced up to the roof. "Come on, I think we're both thinking the same thing."

Climbing the ladder wasn't an easy proposition. The rungs were greasy making for a slippery climb. On the roof the first thing to hit them was the still fresh smell of tar. Apparently, the roof had been repaired to stop leaks. The next thing they saw were five cartons of eggs near the edge. Harry stepped onto the roof and promptly ended up seated on his backside. "Watch your step, this stuff's slick." Oliver's head popped up and he scanned the roof. He pointed to a spot center of the wall almost directly over the dumpster. There was a carton of broken eggs lying open at the ledge. "Looks like skid marks over there." Harry nodded. "Yeah, I think so too. Looks like the poor kid was planning his last prank, it seems it unfortunately was."

Solemnly they climbed down and went to their office to fill out the end of the report. "Harry, this is the second time we were on a case where there wasn't one. I hope you don't plan on making this a habit." They went to the board and marked the case closed then started a new file for their next one.

JACK AND JILL

OSI Agents Harry and Oliver were lazing behind their desks annotating reports and clarifying statements in a leisurely manner. Outside the sun blazed and a light wind blew. Harry opened the window and promptly regretted it when an errant gust blew sheaves of papers onto the floor. With a grunt he bent over and gathered them together. Straightening up he was met with a grin from Oliver whose desk was just out of line with the air flow.

Poised over his desk Harry sorted through the mess of papers. As he tapped them into alignment, he patted them into shape and laid them before him. The top page showed a couple with bandages on their arms and sides. The man had a wrapped bandage on the right side of his shoulder. The caption underneath read Sra. Darnel Wilson and Ms. Penny Lane. Harry read the case history underneath.

Sra Warren Wilson and Ms. Penny Lane had been accosted while walking down King Lane by a person wearing a black face covering. The individual was dressed completely in black. The individual threatened them with a blade and demanded their money. This was speedily given to them and then the individual tossed it aside. They looked steadily at Ms. Lane before stabbing Sra. Wilson. When Ms. Lane tried to shield Sra. Wilson, the individual tried to pull her off with their free hand. Ms. Lane resisted clinging onto Sra. Wilson. The culprit then lunged at Ms. Lane striking her in the right shoulder and continued down piercing her in the right side.

Neither of these people could offer any clue as to the assailant or the reason for the assault. Robbery was not the motive as the individual left the purse and wallet in the bush where they had tossed them.

Assailant remains at large. With no further information case has been assigned as pending further investigation.

The paper was dated a June 15 1987 a week previous. He checked around and no one seemed interested in taking up the case. He laid it in front of Oliver. "What say we take this on. It's a hell of a lot more interesting then shuffling papers." Oliver looked the report over. "Looks like a dead one, nothing to go on." Harry tapped on the paragraph he thought would give a start. "He tried to pull her off Wilson, when she clung to him it seems like it angered him. I'd say he was pulling her off because he was jealous. When he couldn't get her to himself, he stabbed out of anger and frustration." Oliver looked up. "You might be right." He looked down at his own stack of papers and groaned. "Let's put this up to the captain and see if he'll let us take it on."

In the Office of Captain Martin, they went over the case as they saw it and received the clearance to proceed. Stepping outside the office they packed away the rest of the files on their desks and rushed out the door.

As they emerged from the darkness of the office the glare of sunlight made them shade their eyes. They hopped onto a bases shuttle and rode to base housing. Ms. Lane was a civilian who worked as the Base Exchange accountant. Since she was going to be stationed here a long time she had received permission for housing on base. Oliver knocked. When the door opened he introduced Harry and himself. Ushered inside they were seated at the Dining room table and over a cup of coffee and scones she related what happened.

"I really don't know what I can add that isn't in your report already." She drummed her fingers on the table her diamond ring flashing intermittently when the sunlight struck it. Harry grinned, "Congratulations on your recent engagement." She looked up startled. "How do you know my engagement was recent?" Harry's grinned broadened, "Your ring is new judging by its condition and the indent on your finger is fresh. Had you had the ring for longer the indent would have been more permanent. When you grasped your cup, I noticed that the ring moved, your skin sprang up showing the ring was recently acquired."

She held the ring out and admired the play of light shining over it. "Your right Warren just recently asked me to marry him. He gave it to me a couple of days ago." She looked at Harry and her eyebrows puckered. "You see a lot and quick too. Maybe if I try harder, I can think of something to help."

Oliver asked for a list of her acquaintances. "Is there any of the males on this list that is fond of you or might have looked upon you as a possible close friend." She shook her head negatively. "No, they're all from work. I don't go out much and since I met Warren, I don't go out at all unless I'm with him." They asked a few more questions about the assailant, what was he wearing, type of shoes, jewelry worn. Most of this was already in the report but one piece of information that was new regarded the belt. It was blue not black. She remembered when the person moved under the light that the belt stood out. The buckle was smooth and shiny like the belt worn on the blues uniform. She shrugged and apologized for not remembering more. She ran her hands through her red gold hair and frowned. When she said nothing more but sat finger combing her hair Harry and Oliver decided to leave. With a start she rose from the chair and escorted them to the door. "Thanks for the coffee and scones."

Harry waived and pulled Oliver down the path. "A blues belt, maybe they're military, are any of those on her list military?" Oliver looked at the list. "No, all civilians. Seems like they all work at the BX too."

They were on the way to the shuttle stop to go back and get Harry's car to interview Mr. Wilson when their beepers went off. Harry saw in the distance a red call box and rushed to it, Oliver followed at a more leisurely pace. Harry stepped out of the box as Oliver approached. "We have to go back to the office, there were two more attacks last night."

Back at OSI two couples were waiting in the captain's office. The captain rose and excused himself so Harry and Oliver could take over the interviews. The reports they received were almost identical to the ones given by Wilson and Lane. They filled in the reports and thanked the couples for coming in with an assurance that they would investigate the attack thoroughly. The captain returned and escorted the couples out. Harry and Oliver remained, waiting for him. "Well gentlemen, It seems we have an individual on a spree. All these attacks happened in different parts of the base but the MO is the same." Harry looked up from his notes, "What about the fact that all the couples were mixed race?" Oliver was startled, "You mean maybe the guys a racist or something?" Harry shrugged, "maybe, I'm not saying they are I'm just saying it's something to bear in mind." The captain looked thoughtful; "I have heard there is a group of them around. They're keeping pretty quiet since their numbers are few. It could be that, but I have a feeling it isn't." Harry was set to object, but Oliver laid a hand on his shoulder.

After the meeting they went back over the notes looking for a lead. Harry went to a map and pinned the locations of the attacks. "Looks like the locations are random. There's no way to stake out an area and wait." Oliver went to the board and looked at the pinned areas. "no pattern except they seem to be secluded areas a couple might use for a rendezvous."

For the next few hours Harry and Oliver visited the areas in question. All were open areas with benches and heavily grassed. Harry was annoying Oliver with his Sherlock routine. Harry was peering into bushes, examining the ground under the benches, picking up cigarette butts. "Harry, security forces have already gone over the place and collected any evidence." Harry stood, his face red from squatting and looking under the bench. "I'm just checking around to see if anything got missed."

Oliver snorted, "What was the idea of your declamation on Lanes ring? Seemed a little showing off to me." Harry sat down to defend himself. "I did it to show were observant and intuitive. People aren't inclined to lie to you if they think you can tell straight off if they're lying." Oliver agreed, "Save stuff like that when we're interviewing the assailant not the victim."

Oliver sat on the bench to do some thinking. Harry wandered around to do his. Oliver opened up to Harry. "What I don't get is that the people were attacked but not killed. From what we're being told the attacker was in a rage but still in control enough to inflict wounds. Harry agreed and offered a reason. "maybe they are not normally aggressive and something drove them to the point of aggression, they still might shrink from murder at the last."

Oliver agreed, shrugged, stretched and checking his watch mentioned it was clocking out time. "Can I drop you off home?" Harry shook his head, "Nope, they have a dance tonight at the club so I figure since I'm already in a suit I might just head over there for a while. "Have fun," Oliver stopped and turned around, "I thought you told me you didn't know how to dance." Harry acknowledged this with a shrug. "True, guess I'll just go and ogle all the pretty prettys." Oliver slid into his car and waved goodnight to Harry.

It was a cool evening and Harry was glad of the wool jacket of his suit. Reaching into his pocket he pulled out a packet of Dunhills and inhaled deeply. As he walked he let little whisps of smoke trickle out like the puffs of a steam locomotive. He blew out the rest so that it plumed as he whistled loudly. Laughing softly to himself he walked the rest of the way to the club mimicking a train the entire way.

Opening the door to the club he surveyed the interior. To his right were a few inexpensive slots. He had avoided these ever since one of his first pay checks was lost in there. He gave it a wide berth and walked into the large bar room where the dance was to be held. It was still early so he got a pint and sat at a front corner table. From here he could watch as people entered as well as having a commanding view of the floor. He sauntered back to the bar leaning against it and talked to John the bartender.

John was wiping up the bar, "I didn't expect to see you here tonight Harry, you said you didn't dance." Harry took a long pull at his pint, "I don't but that doesn't mean I can't enjoy some company though." John's lips tightened. "Oh, so you're here for a pick up then." Harry emptied his pint, "nope, just here to be with people. I don't believe in a one night stand and for all I know I could get orders soon. It wouldn't be fair to start something serious and not be able to take her with me when I leave." Johns face relaxed as he poured Harry another pint. "There aren't many that'll come in tonight shares your view. It's just like it was in WW II. Bunch of Yanks come in and next thing you know there aren't any girls left for our boys. I lost my best girl to a yank a long time ago." A reminiscent look came into Johns eyes. He shook his head sadly, "Still hurts like hell when I think of her." Harry sympathized sincerely and bought him a pint.

Resuming his seat he watched the guy's from the dorms file in. The noise rose as folks talked and shot pool on one of the tables at the side. As they drank and talked they cast surreptitious eyes towards the doorway in expectation of that which was to come. Around 2000 the sound of chatter and laughter was heard from the entranceway. A bevy of beauties waltzed in and began to mingle with the males. Soon the area around the bar was engulphed as the men brought drinks for the ladies. John was hard pressed to fill the orders. He rushed back and forth from tap to tap as he poured pints and half pints. From the speakers on the wall a selection of dance music poured forth and some advanced to the open spaces.

John sat with Harry and surveyed the dancers. "Can't say much for what they call dancing these days." John muttered as he looked over the dancers. Harry stifled a laugh, "You prefer the jitterbug or swing?" John looked shocked, "Now what do you know about the jitterbug?" "Not much but I hear it was pretty energetic." A young lady approached the table where they were sitting, she was attractive and diminutive, she had a gentle smile as she approached. John nudged Harry, "How's your resolve now?" Harry began to rise as she approached, she smiled at Harry but approached John. "I was wondering if you'd teach me a dance you know." John rose with dignity and placed her arm in his. As they approached the dance floor swing music issued forth over the speakers.

Harry rested his glass on the table and watched John and the young lady. They started slow as John explained the dance to her then the floor was cleared as they took off. Swing and the jitterbug apparently were very energetic and though John was in his sixties he still had retained his vigor. As they twirled and flew around the floor several enterprising couples joined in. Though not as adept as John and his partner they nevertheless were in for the win. By the time the music ended there were quite a few who had joined in and the floor was crowded with laughing dancers and applauding watchers.

John bought his companion a drink and she went back to the milling throng. Harry complimented John on his dancing. "You've still got a bit of style about you." John wiped his brow, "I remember being able to do that all evening, can't go as long as I used to now." He smiled as the young lady came back into view and waved at them. John's eyes got misty momentarily as he watched her dancing with a young American. "She looks a bit like my Mary. Same long curls in her hair and about the same size. I wonder where she is now." Harry sat quietly as John was lost in reminiscences.

A few customers came up to the bar and John roused himself to deal with their orders. Harry ordered a half pint to top off. He spun it out a little longer then walked over to lodging. Two and a half pints was his limit and he wasn't going to drive intoxicated. Getting a ticket for drunk driving as an OSI agent would look just great. He paid his eight dollars for the night and went to bed.

Back at the club John was announcing last call and beginning to clean up. He saw the young lady he had danced with heading out with a young man headed for the dorms. She gave him a cheery farewell albeit with a slightly intoxicated look about her. He shook his head in disappointment and continued to clean up. He locked the bar and then turned off most of the lights. A few were left on so Security could see all was well when they made their rounds. John locked the front door then made his way to his car. It was a long walk to the fence line just passed the single officers dorms. He liked to stroll in the evening and catch the fresh air after all the smoke and heat of the club.

He was passing the last dorm when he heard a snuffle and whimper to his left. On the stoop was the young lady he had met earlier. "Hattie? That you child?" She wiped her eyes and blew her nose. "Yes, it's me. She rose and looked both upset and embarrassed. "I went to his room and He wanted to but I didn't, He, she couldn't get the words out to John so passed over that part. "Anyways he just now kicked me out!" John's jaw clenched and his fingers closed into a fist. Hattie was still snuffling, "He told me to find my own way home, the cabs and busses won't be back for at least an hour. I'm cold and tired and now I've got a long walk to get home!"

John wrapped his coat around her shoulders and escorted her to his car. "You really don't mind?" She looked up at him with so pathetic a countenance that John's heart gave a double thump. "No, I don't mind." As they drove out the gate and headed to Beck Row John tried to find out anything she could tell him about the Lieutenant. She couldn't remember his room number or even which Dorm she had come out from. She admitted that she had drunk more then she should have. "All I wanted to do was have a good time," She whimpered. "You don't do this often do you." She shook her head. A few of her girlfriends had induced her to join them on base for some free booze and dancing. They did it all the time and told her it would be a blast. She slumped lower in her seat. "It was fun at the beginning, and I enjoyed dancing with you." She patted his hand on the stick shift of the Austin Mini Mini. "I guess I won't be doing that again anyways." John muttered "Good," under his breath.

He pulled up to a small cottage and escorted her to the door. She invited him inside but he courteously declined with an admonition that she go straight to bed and get some rest. The rest of the way home John grumbled to himself.

Harry woke the next morning with only a slight headache and crossed the street heading to Mickey's Tea Bar for some breakfast. As he passed his car, he changed his mind and went into Mildenhall to the small tea shop he frequented where he could get a full breakfast. Sated he went over to Oliver's house to pick him up. "Had a good time last night?" Oliver inquired as he finished off his own meal. "Harry poured himself a cup of tea and sat down opposite Oliver to tell him of his night of debauchery.

Seated in the front room they discussed the case so far. Oliver handed over a couple of more reports the captain had acquired the day before. They all were similar to the ones that had been received earlier. "The captain did mention that your idea of a racist slant will have to be set aside since out of the three new cases two were both white and one Asian." Harry shrugged as Oliver pulled out a small base map and placed three more x's at the locations of the latest attacks.

Harry studied the map looking for some continuity, The attacks looked random but there had to be something tying them together. He started numerating what he could. All the attacks were fanned out across the base. The people were chosen at random and not based on race, age or gender. He scratched his head. "I don't get it, what are we missing." Oliver turned the map around. He took a ruler and drew a line down from the most center attack. Then he drew a line down linking the rest of the attacks to the center line. Within the lines were three possible points of interest.

"If we use this as our guide then we have three starting points, The fitness center, the club and the rec center." Harry agreed and looked at the reports once more. All the days of the attacks were on a Tuesday or Friday and all were after 2200. He added the notation onto the map. "I'd say we should eliminate the fitness center. Doesn't fit the time scheme." Oliver posited. Harry agreed. "What goes on at the Rec Center on Tuesday that continues into the night?" Oliver inquired. Harry pulled out his notebook and flipped through the pages until he came on his notes of things to do on base. "Tuesday and Friday at the rec center is bingo night. It usually ends about 2100." "Harry, I don't think bingo is going to draw much from off base. It's got to be the club. That brings many a fair maiden from the town here and plenty stay to the end of the evening *or longer*." Harry checked the reports again.

"I think your right, look at the ranks on the males and none on the females." Oliver refilled his cup and leaned back in his chair. "I think were onto something here. He sank into a deep revery. Suddenly he went into the kitchen and placed a call. He came back in and sat down on the edge of his chair. "I put a call through to Ms. Martin. She's on her way over." Harry cocked an eyebrow, "Who's she when she's at home." Oliver lay back again, "She's only recently come to OSI, works in the photo lab and is the resident expert in photographic analysis. She's a British civilian and really knows her stuff. It's a shame we didn't have her on our first case together. It's funny, she's almost thirty but looks like she's in her late teens or early twenties. I'm surprised you haven't seen her by now."

A rap on the door and Oliver rose to let his guest in. Harry rose as she entered, to his surprise he had seen Ms. Martin after all, but not at work. He shook her hand, "Didn't I meet you at the club a while ago?" She nodded and smiled. "You were sitting with John when I asked him to teach me to dance. He really knows how too. He's a nice chap." Harry nodded agreement. "I heard he picked you up and took you home when one of the lieutenants was being an asshole and kicked you out in the middle of the night." She took the cup of tea Oliver had poured out for her and added sugar to it. "It wasn't quite like that. The Lt had been buying drink after drink for some poor child and she was at the point I was worried for her. I seduced him into thinking I was already fairly drunk and would be a better conquest then her, Once I had his full attention I went to the bar and asked John to call her a taxi giving him a pound to pay for it." He ensured she got away alright. After a while the lieutenant wanted to leave. I let him lead me out. I waved to John on the way. Halfway to the officer dorms I picked a fight with him and by the time we got to where he lived, he wasn't interested in me anymore. I was sitting on the steps resting for a bit when John came along. I gave him a sob story and he drove me home. Wrong of me probably but I didn't want to hang around waiting for a taxi to come back."

Harry lit her cigarette. She smoked for a while in silence while Oliver meditated on how to put his request to her. When her cigarette was finished, she turned to Oliver. "What is it you want me to do?" The abruptness shook him. He quickly regained his poise and put it forward in a straightforward manner.

"We believe we have discovered where the attacker is making their start from. We believe they go to the club, chooses some couple that they decide for reasons of their own are, shall we say, are objectionable to him out of jealousy or some other reason. Our opinion is that he is against military and civilian females getting together, we want you to serve as bait. Pick a military person at the dance, convince him to take you out for an evening stroll and we will be following ready to act if you are attacked." She gave the proposal careful consideration. She was looking alternatively at Harry and Oliver speculatively. "I agree, however with this proviso, I want to enter as I have, on my own as if I have come in from town. I want to approach Harry here and inveigle him to buy me a few drinks then have him escort me out." She looked at Harry and a slight smile crossed her lips.

Oliver was curious, "Why Harry?" Harry was just as curious though the prospect was certainly not unpleasant to him. She ticked off her points on her fingers, "One he's OSI so he'd be safest to do this with in case of emergency. Two, I have seen him previously when he was at the table with John and three," Here her smile broadened, *"he's kind of a cutie."* Harry choked on his tea and turned red with embarrassment but readily agreed to be bait as well.

She left with the assurance that everything would be prepared before the next dance. Harry and Oliver called in to the captain and described what they wanted to do. Receiving approval, they set in motion their plans for capturing the assailant.

Tuesday arrived and all was set for the trap to be sprung. The captain had stationed agents at five of the six sites. Harry and Hattie had been in contact working over the "script" for the evening. Harry arrived at the club early and took his customary seat at the corner. John welcomed him warmly and brought him a pint as well as one for himself. "I don't know why you come to these dances when I have never seen you on the floor." Harry shrugged, "Guess I'm waiting to be asked." John spit a bit of beer back into the glass. He looked at Harry with a grin. "Good luck with that." He finished off his beer then went behind the counter as people starting ambling in.

The place started filling up and there was still no sign of Hattie. She finally showed half an hour after the dance started. She waived hello to John then started making the rounds of the floor. She approached a young man who had been standing near the speaker with a sour expression as he watched people pair off. Harry had seen him before and was not surprised he never got chosen. There was something about his demeaner that was decidedly off putting. He rarely smiled and when he approached a female was usually brushed off. Hattie saw where Harry was looking and made a beeline for him. The look of surprise on the man's face when Hattie asked him to dance was almost comical. On the dance floor it could hardly be said that they danced together. He jumped and spun all around, did splits and hand walks until Hattie had had enough. She thanked him for the "dance" and went to the bar ordering a half pint for herself.

The airman followed her to the bar and insisted on buying her another half pint. She thanked him but declined. He became insistent and telling her he'd buy her all the drinks she wanted. She gave a firmer refusal which he ignored. Harry felt it might be time to intervene. Approaching the bar he tapped the insistent gentleman on the arm. He angrily spun around. Harry excused himself and eased the fella away from the bar.

He addressed himself to Hattie, "I didn't see you when you came in, Sorry I wasn't able to pick you up my car's starter is still out." Hattie's face positively beamed on Harry, "I was looking for you out on the dance floor and passing the time taking a few turns. Where have you been hiding." Harry pointed to the seat in the corner. Hattie eagerly picked up her drink and joined him in the corner. With a sour look the airman handed her a piece of paper with his name and number on it. "Let me know when you want to trade up." He snorted, glared at Harry and went back to his place. Leaning against the wall he pounded softly on it with clenched fists.

Harry got himself another pint and bought one for John inviting him to join them. Seated, John asked Hattie if she wanted him to toss out the airman who annoyed her. "No, at least in here you can keep an eye on him. She looked towards the door as another group came in. Amongst them was Oliver. He didn't acknowledge them but went to a group of girls and picked a partner for the next dance. Harry stole a look at the paper before Hattie placed it into a pocket. The airman's name was Steve. No last name given but Harry was pretty sure he had seen him a time or two working at lodging. It wouldn't be much trouble to lay hands on him if needs be.

Harry wiled away a short time talking with Hattie and John when John wasn't busy serving. John seemed a little tense that Hattie was becoming friendly with Harry. Hattie invited Harry out on the floor and Harry reluctantly agreed. The song was a slow one and Harry and Hattie danced close together. Her close warmth and the soft fragrance she wore raised feelings in Harry he hadn't had in a while. She looked up into his eyes as they danced, and a warm smile crossed her lips. By the wall Steve inwardly seethed as he watched them dance closely. Hattie murmured to Harry to kiss her as it might make someone jealous. Harry cupped her chin in his hand and kissed her. When they broke, she sighed and placed her head on his chest as they continued to dance. Harry wasn't sure if Hattie was serious or simply a very accomplished actress but either way he was enjoying her company

On the wall Steve was thumping harder on the wall with his fists and glaring at Harry and Hattie. Behind the bar John was disappointed in Harry and concerned for Hattie. Oliver moved to a space where he could overlook the floor and see if anyone was concentrating on anyone particular. He noticed that the only focus was on Harry and Hattie. Steve and John were unwavering in their attention. Harry led Harriet back to the table. She declined his offer of another drink and John was grateful he didn't hear Harry press her. Harry spun out his beer for another half hour. "You want to walk out for a bit and get some air." Harry said it loud enough to be heard but not so loud as to be unnatural. Hattie rose and put her arm through his and they walked outside. Several people followed as well and there was a scrum at the door as people filed out into the moonlight. Among the leaving throng was Steve. Oliver followed soon after. He knew the route Harry was taking and it would take ten minutes for them to be in position. As Oliver left, he heard John yell out "last call" and hurrying to close the place down and leave himself.

Harry and Hattie were headed past the bowling alley to the large field beyond. This area was dimly lit and the moonlight filtered through the trees making dappled patterns on the ground. Harry lay his jacket down next to a tree for Hattie to sit on. He sat on the grass and leaned back. Hattie leaned on Harry's arm and waited. If anything was going to happen, now would be the time. Five minutes passed with no interruption; Hattie was getting a feeling nothing would happen that night. "Want to call it a night and try again next dance?" "Let's wait a bit longer he whispered." From the right came a low growl and their view of the moon was blocked by a figure covered in black and the face hidden by a ski mask. The only visible object was the sliver of a blade.

"You make a cute couple, I hope you had a good evening cause it's going to be your last." growled the individual with the knife, Harry started to rise and received a kick to the stomach, Hattie screamed in spite of herself. Harry recovered his breath and made a lunge for the black shrouded body. As they toppled Harry felt the knife penetrate his shoulder. Hattie leapt up and had the attacker in a choke hold, with her other hand she ripped off the mask. Harry expected to see Steve's glaring countenance. What was revealed was certainly glaring but wasn't Steve. Oliver ran up and assisted to subdue the writhing and flailing attacker. Once standing and still, the attacker was revealed to be a female and a very angry one at that. Hattie wrapped her scarf around the knife in Harry's shoulder to keep it in place until they could get Harry to the hospital. Oliver led his captive away, her bitter cursing fading in the distance. Harry's car was nearby, and Hattie drove him to Lakenheath to be seen to. She quailed a bit when she realized she had to pop the clutch but needs must when the devil drives.

Harry was repaired quickly but required to remain for a couple of days. Oliver and Hattie arrived soon after breakfast with an update. Oliver flipped out his notebook, "You know I really thought it was going to be Steve or just possibly John." Hattie and Harry agreed. "Her name is A1C Francie Jessup and she's originally from Cleveland Ohio. Been here for about seven months. Apparently, she was pissed because with all these British local ladies coming on base at the dances she wasn't getting in on the action. She finally went off the rails and started following couples and slashing them. I was following Steve out since he was in the group that left when you did. He got as far as the playground by the Youth Center and when he started swinging on the swings, I realized I was on the wrong tack. Seems like you two had things well in hand by the time I arrived." He rubbed his shins, "Damn, what a wildcat!"

Hattie kissed Harry on the forehead, "Bye hero, rest up. I'll drop by to see you later." She headed out. Oliver rose and stretched. "Guess I'll be heading back too. Take care of yourself. Oh' you going to be o.k. to push start your mini tomorrow or should I swing by and give you a bump start." Harry laughed and promised to get his starter fixed when he got out. Rubbing his shoulder, he asked Oliver to swing by for that bump.

WHERE THERE IS SMOKE THERE IS FIRE

Harry woke to a slight smell of smoke. He rose from his bed at lodging and got dressed quickly. Calling the desk he asked if they knew anything. Negative. He walked around the outside. Having a room at the back of lodging he walked out directly in front of the dumpsters. To the right of the door was a red cannister for dumping cigarettes into. A few were still lit and sending out wreaths of smoke. "Probably what I smelt" he thought but did a complete walkaround just to be on the safe side. Arriving again at the back door he extinguished the cigarettes completely and went back to his room.

He washed his hands and sat for a bit reading a paperback he had brought with him. He sniffed the air and still smelt smoke. He sniffed at his hands and clothes. Wasn't him. He went back outside and checked again. He found a stick and started poking around in the dumpsters. Shuffling through discarded papers the smell of smoke grew stronger and a sudden burst of flames erupted as air was introduced to embers. Harry sped to the hose attached to the wall and sprayed the flames. He doused the dumpster thoroughly and stirred everything to ensure the fire was out completely. He went to the front desk to report what he found. They scratched a note in the pass on log and thanked him for putting it out. He retired to his room to catch up on his sleep.

Rising he looked at the clock and realized he had fifteen minutes to get to work, A quick wash and brush meant he was at work and at his desk on time. Oliver had preceded him and was already going over some notes. Harry got up to get a coffee to jump start his day. When he sat down Oliver was looking at him judicially. "What happened last night that you had to hurry getting here?" Harry looked up, "How did you know I had to hurry here?" Oliver eyed him again critically, "Well, while you combed your hair you made no attempt to trim the scraggle from your beard. This is something you are normally careful to do. I also noticed when you arrived that your shoes were lacking their accustomed bright shine. Oh, and your shirt tale is hanging out." Harry stood and corrected the mentioned offenses sans the beard. "I was up early over at lodging. I smelled smoke and didn't see anything the first time checking except a few cig butts that were still smoldering. When I still smelt smoke, I checked the dumpster. Something was doing a slow burn under all the papers and when I moved things around with a stick it flamed up. I got it put out and reported it to the front desk." Harry gulped some coffee and looked over the roster for any details for the day.

Oliver was still staring at Harry. "So, what started the fire?" Harry looked up, "I dunno, I just wanted to get back to bed." Oliver rose and put on his jacket. "Come on." He tugged at Harry's sleeve. As they passed the captains door Oliver called in saying they were headed out. As they walked Harry was inquiring why they were headed back to lodging. Oliver stopped and looked at Harry, concern in his eyes. "You alright pal? You're not acting like the analyst I know. By your own admission you discover a fire that was smoldering under a stack of waste papers. Once the fire was out you made no attempt to see why there were smoldering embers in the dumpster. Granted, someone could have tossed a cigarette in and it started something burning but with an ash can right there it's doubtful. Normally your inquisitive nature would have caused you to investigate, the fact that you did not and that you arrived in your aforementioned state leads me to deduce you have something urgent or of great interest on your mind. Might I hazard a guess it is Hattie?" Harry actually blushed." Maybe a little we have been seeing each other once in a while, or it could just be that I was woken early and subsequently over slept" At lodging they went to the dumpsters. Unfortunately, the trash collectors had gotten there ahead of them.

Oliver shrugged, "Oh well, I just wanted to see if there was anything to see." They walked the seven blocks back to work each lost in his own thoughts. Back at their desks they went over the roster again. In the distance they heard a siren emerging from the fire station. The blur of red passed their window as the fire truck sped down the street.

Harry and Oliver joined the rush of people going outside to see where the truck was heading. As a matter of habit Harry grabbed an evidence case on the way. "Looks like the Commissary, want to go intrude?" Oliver was already speeding down the street. Harry was game and put on a burst of speed catching up to Oliver just as they approached the commissary. The security police looked at the slightly disheveled and out of breath pair who requested entrance to the scene and was about to rebuff them. The badges they proffered gained them the access they sought.

At the rear of the building was a smoldering dumpster. The firemen had done quick work putting it out. Security was there as well and they joined forces to determine the cause. Allowing for things to cool down they took pictures of the dumpsters insides and contents. The still smoldering remains were brought out and sorted through. A few wax covered boxes, the purple dimpled cardboard used to hold apples in place in the boxes, a few wooden crates, bits of flyers and posters. All the items were examined and photographed until the dumpster was empty. Oliver took samples of some of the items to see if any accelerant had been applied. He doubted it though as there was enough wax on the boxes to act on their own.

Harry put on a plastic jumpsuit and climbed into the container. Pulling a flashlight from his vest pocket he peered into the corners and crevice's. He took some pictures of one of the corners and scrapped some flaked paint off the sides, He took close up pictures and some more scrapings at four different levels. Oliver stood outside the dumpster and watched Harry scraping away. When done Harry climbed out and divested himself of the coverall. Oliver was approving of Harrys actions "Now that's the way to do it. To bad you weren't of a mind to do that at Lodging. We might have had a comparison to work with." Harry sheepishly agreed he hadn't been in good form last night.

Back to OSI Headquarters they turned in the evidence and film to be analyzed. An hour later Mattie dropped the pictures by the desk and sat down. "Oliver, I couldn't get much from the items in the dumpster except for these two, The dark tiny spots coincide with the section of dumpster Harry photographed." She looked at Harry. "Oliver tells me your good at analysis, what did you see that made you take pictures and samples?" Harry pulled the photos he had taken and sorted them. The fire was started on the left hand side and moved to the right where the majority of the refuse was dumped. Something was placed at the left rear corner." He pointed to a mark halfway up the picture. "You can see that the fat on the wall is mixed with smoke but lighter than what happened on the right side. There is also a clear striped area meaning that a heat source was slowly burning down a distance of three inches. From there it flared to high heat and expelled sparks. The slow burn and light ash I would suggest was compressed wood similar to a punk. Down further was something similar to a sparkler only with larger sparks, high heat and metal shavings were used to set off the fire.

Hattie was impressed. "You don't disappoint, I better be careful or you could take my place." She turned to Oliver, "as far as I can tell, his reading is correct and for the same reasons. The dispersal pattern on the wall and on the items from the dumpster show the splay pattern and distance denoting the size and force of the, for lack of a better term, sparkler. This shows the fire was premeditated and that the arsonist is creative and intelligent. I passed the lab on my way here and they'll have their findings in a bit. Mind if I hang out and hear?" Oliver did a lunch run to Mikeys and came back with a sack of beef burgers, fries and sodas.

Over lunch they read the Stars and Stripes. Harry had the local entertainment ads, Mattie had the local sports scores and Oliver had the comics. Harry was hoping to find something to take Mattie to. She had spoken more than once about wanting to see a show. Their first had taken a two hour drive to get to Leighton Buzzard for a performance of Cosi Fan Tutti. He was hoping for something a little closer. "Hattie, it says here they're putting on Damn Yankees at Lakenheath Rec Center.

Want to see some amateur dramatics?" She maintained her professionalism since they were in the office and agreed to go, but there was a bright light in her eyes that betrayed her eagerness. Oliver looked up to see them lost in each other's eyes. "Oh for Christ's sake, you're like a couple of kids." Oliver muttered.

Harry finished off his cold fries as Lou from analysis came over and joined them. He helped himself to the leftover fries as he went over his findings. "From the samples you provided the chip from bag one contained elements of wood smoke in high concentrations. The other bags contained potassium perchlorate, aluminum, and dextrin, there were also aluminum hydroxide, calcium hydrogen phosphates, calcium carbonate, silica and hydroxyapatite. Fluoride plus some sort of abrasive. "Fluoride?| Oliver asked, "sounds like toothpaste!" Lou congratulated Oliver on his scientific acumen. "That's just what it was. Seems your friend mixed the first part and second and made themselves a pretty large sparkler. No wonder it set off the dumpster. The large bits of aluminum would have stayed hot long enough to start it." "Would you say it was something anyone could do?" Harry wondered. Lou gave this careful consideration. "I'd say possible but not probable. He finished off the rest of the fries and went back to the lab. Harry added everything to the file and relaxed. "Well, were getting closer, now we just wait for the next one." Mattie left after ensuring that they would be going to the play tomorrow.

Harry was doing some research at the library. In the reference section were reports from plenty of Government agencies. He found the FBI section and went over the reports on arson and arsonists. He wanted to know how often an arsonist would set fires. It seemed to depend on motivation. If it was for profit it was usually a one time deal. Revenge might happen a few times in the victims home, workplace, car, etc.. If it was for the pleasure of watching the fires it would usually happen after a lapse of a couple of days. Usually, the perpetrator would be one of the crowd of watchers.

Harry considered the two fires. They could have been started the same way. He might have intervened and put out the Lodging fire while it was still smoldering and hadn't reached the sparkler yet. With no data from that fire they were at a standstill. He walked outside and decided to take a walk before heading home. Walking was good for the appetite and he wanted to go to the Kings Head for a dinner of roast, Yorkshire pudding and green peas. The thought of it sent his gastric juices surging. He walked around the outskirts of the base towards the waste dump. The dump wasn't his destination, but it was about midway. "Odd, I smell smoke but don't see any fire." He hoofed it as fast as he could to the dump. A large collection of pallets were burning. The odd thing was that the flame was purple. Suddenly the fire burst as if a jerry can of gas had been thrown on it. He went to the phone attached to the office hut and called it in. There was a small explosion and the flame changed to green. As the firetruck approached another explosion and the flame changed to red. The firemen worked quickly and covered the flame with foam. Harry wondered why they hadn't used water. When the fire was out he asked the fire chief about that. "In this place you never know what's on fire or could be hidden inside it. We use a suppression foam here as a matter of course. It's good for any kind of fire so we're sure to get it out.

Security Forces were not far behind and closed off the area so they could do their job. He waived to SSgt Jarvis as he came out from the far side of the pallets. He waived back beckoning Harry over. "I assumed you'd want to look around a bit. Harry walked around the stack of smoldering wood. "Can I borrow a bag if you have one?" SSgt Jarvis pulled one from the inside of the firetruck and handed it to Harry. Rolled small it became large enough to fit into a 55 gal drum. Jarvis laughed as he retrieved it and handed over a much smaller zip lock bag. "What'd you find?" "A sealed packet that has a layer of what looks like charcoal or maybe it could be something like Pyrodex black powder with a white powder layered on top." A tap on his shoulder made Harry turn around. A SP was at his side. "We'll take care of that for you and let you know what it is." Harry left and let security take care of it. Cutting the rest of his walk short he drove into town for his dinner.

Friday started off busy. Harry and Oliver had the reports from the Security Forces as well as from their own analysts waiting for them. Each taking one they perused them. Harry was fascinated by the section describing the white powder. It was straight magnesium sulphate. The black was pyrodex. Harry placed a call to Pyrotechnics Guild International. He wanted a list of any licensed practitioners in the local area. They promised to have the information to him within an hour. Oliver was impressed, "how did you know who to call so quickly?" Harry pulled out his own certificate. "I used to do pyrotechnic magic in my teens."

Oliver put down his report. "Did you ever screw up?" Harry's face paled as the memory came flooding back. Oh yeah, It's also why I don't drink like I used too. He lit a cigarette and his hand shook as he began his tale. "I was working at a gas station and talking to the other mechanics about one of my favorite tricks. We had been drinking a six pack and shots and I was a light weight so it affected me pretty hard. My trick was that I would place a bowl filled with lighter fluid on a table, dip my hand in and then light it on fire. I'd hold it up for a bit then fling the fire off sending it streaming to a wore frame box covered in Flash paper. It was a great effect and always made an impression. I always had a gel I would put on first so it didn't get into my pores. They wanted to see it so since we didn't have lighter fluid they poured some gas over my hand in the sink. I lit it and for a moment didn't feel anything. I flung it off and it streamed towards the bay door. I tried to put it out off my hand but the rags were oily and caught fire. One of the guys pulled me to the sing and turned on the water, The fire ran down from my hand into the sink which burst into a fireball. Luckily somebody dumped cat litter over me and put out me and the sink. Only then did we realize we could have set off the tanks for the torch right next to the sink. After that I gave up incendiary magic and drinking too for a while.

Oliver whistled. "That could have ended nastily. So you think the arsonist might be a pyrotech?" Harry nodded, "It's likely considering how he's setting off the fires and that the fire changed colors. They started small and seem to be building up one by one." Oliver said he didn't like the sound of that since the pallet fire was fairly large what would the next be like." In Harry's car they did a drive around to see if there was anywhere with a large pile of material that would appeal to their arsonist. Nothing was visible. Harry drove Oliver home and then went to get scrubbed up for his evening with Hattie.

A short drive to Lakenheath, Dinner at the club and they were seated at the rec center for the eight o'clock show. To Harry and Hattie, the star was MSgt Reynolds who played Applegate/the Devil. His devilish aspects made the show. He made cigarettes appear then lit them by brushing his finger over the top, he lit a fire in the fireplace by sending a stream of fire from his fingertip and he made one of the contracts disappear in a burst of flames. For an amateur production it was very well done and the applause went on for a long time. On the way to Hattie's place she thanked Harry for a lovely evening. "One thing though, I do wish you'd fix the starter. It makes me nervous when you push start then jump in while the car's still moving." Harry absently agreed to change the starter as soon as he found the time. "So, never" muttered Hattie. She realized that for some odd reason Harry liked to push start his car so fixing it wasn't going to be a priority.

There were no more fires over the weekend. On Monday Harry suggested that they visit Lakenheath rec center and talk to Mr. Scott Wagner. He was the one who handled the pyrotechnics for the show. He was also on the list of licensed members locally. The rec center was closed but people were inside. Harry knocked incessantly until the door was opened. "Sorry but were prepping for the show later, you'll have to come back then." In unison the badges were flashed and they gained admittance. They were shown onto the stage and introduced to Mr. Wagner.

"Hi gents, I hope this won't take long, I've got a lot to set up and not a lot of time. My assistant got called into his shop and he's left me high and dry." "You work while we talk. Were curious about where you were yesterday at 1730." He called into the wings. "Allison, what time was I here yesterday?" Allison poked her head out, three til seven. You were fixing the flash boxes and setting up the vials for Morgan." Her head popped back behind the wing curtain. "Morgan's my assistant, He wants to get licensed but has a lot to learn. I had to start premeasuring the mixes. He wants to impress me so he tries to make the flashes bigger then what they need to be and over packs the smoke box. It's good that he's interested in this, but he has to learn control. People can get hurt if you use to much mag in a flash box" "Where does Morgan work?" Harry asked as he brought out his notebook. "At the Chapel, he's a chaplains assistant." "You say he should be there now?" "That's where he said he was headed an hour ago, seems the chaplain needed some files and for him to arrange for a baptism."

Harry and Oliver thanked Mr. Wagner for his time and sped off to the chapel. At the reception desk they were informed that Morgan hadn't been in that day. Driving back to Mildenhall Harry expressed his concerns. "I don't think the next will be on Mildenhall but at Lakenheath. Oliver agreed. If it is Morgan then he wants to do the big one where Wagner can see it. In the office they put a call in to speak to Wagner. "Could you please check your supplies and tell us if anything is missing?" Wagner placed the phone down and checked the firesafe. They could hear things clanging and being shuffled around. When he returned, he sounded agitated. "There sure is something missing, two canisters of Pyrodex, a pack each of Magnesium Sulfate, Strontium Chloride, and Copper Chloride." "And what colors would they change the flame to?" "White, red and blue." Oliver thanked Mr. Wagner with the assurance they would look into it.

Harry retrieved a couple of binoculars for Oliver and himself. He grabbed a couple of Bricks from the charging box. They headed back to Lakenheath. Oliver was in the passenger's seat looking over a map of the base. We've got until nightfall to find where he's building his fire. The only clear spot on base is across from the bowling center. It's clearly visible from the rec center and if he's trying to impress Mr. Wagner, he's going to want to give him a front row seat.

Back on Lakenheath they received permission to go onto the roof of the bowling center. From there they had an eagle eye view of the open field. In the field and to the right forward corner they spotted someone erecting a bonfire. What amazed them was that he was doing so in plain view. Harry mentioned that maybe he was operating under the assumption that if you look like you belong there, people will assume you do. Scanning the area where the bonfire was being constructed, they noticed yellow tape surrounding the area and warning signs strategically placed at 50 yards distance from the center. Harry slid down to where the ladder was and climbed down while Oliver kept watch with a brick at his side. (Note: A brick is what the very large rectangle walkie talkies were called.)

Harry called into the Fire department to see if Morgan had clearance to build a fire in that area. A check and he received a negative response. A quick call to security and within moments three squad cars had arrived. Morgan was swiftly taken into custody and the bonfire dismantled. Harry was impressed at the ingenuity in its construction despite himself. It was made so that the center would fire first then burst into red flame, second would burn and then change to white at a lower level and the third would flame blue. Oliver was ashamed to admit it but he kind of wanted to see it go up. It would have been impressive. It might even have gotten Wagner to put Morgan up for membership in the guild after all.

REYNOLDS WRAPPED

Harry and Oliver were called into the captain's office. On the way they did a check at the full-length mirror to ensure they looked presentable. A knock on the door and they were requested to enter. Standing before his desk they wondered why they had been summonsed. The captain offered them a seat. "I'm pleased with the work you two have accomplished. Harry I'm very pleased Oliver was able to bring you over from services, you two make a good team. I've decided to reward you both with a special assignment. How'd you both like a trip to Lowry Air Force Base in Colorado." He grinned at the look of enthusiasm on their faces. "Harry, I need you to go into the head and shave your beard and mustache off." Harry almost came to tears, he had become fond of his facial hair and felt it made him looked older and distinguished. With a faltering step he took the proffered electric razor and went to defile himself.

The man who returned looked much younger than the one who had left. Harry had a youthful face when smooth and looked younger than his 25 years. "Just as I thought," commented the captain. "Harry, we had a call from the Lowry services schoolhouse. I understand this was your tech school after basic training." Harry agreed, "I went for three level but I didn't go there for five level. I received that by cooking Dinner and Midnight meal by myself." The captain was interested, "Just out of curiosity for how many people." "Just three hundred and fifty for Dinner and about half that for Midnight not including the grill line." The captain was impressed. "You cooked for that many by yourself and worked the grill?" Harry shrugged, "yeah, I did it once to get my five level then they said because I could do it, I would work Dinner and Midnight on my own from then on." Oliver laughed at how Harry got suckered into working the late shift.

The captain continued, "Well you're going to get a chance to go to five level school now." Harry leaned forward to learn more. It was obvious that he wasn't going to go and just learn to cook. "There have been complaints about drugs and alcohol abuse in Service training. I want to send you both to find out who's dealing the drugs. Security isn't able to find out and it's bad there." Oliver was set to object, "Why can't they send someone stateside, why pick us?" "We're the only OSI section that has a Services trained person. Harry can slide in and has the knowledge to blend." He turned to Harry, "Do you still have your cook whites and paraphernalia?" "Their hanging in my closet still starched and pressed." "Better go see if they still fit, come back in, make sure the whole uniform is complete."

An hour later and Harry came back dressed for inspection. He was thankful that he kept himself in trim. The uniform still fit well. Captain Wilson walked around him, "looks good, but were going to reduce your rank to Senior Airman for the duration of this mission. You'll fit in better and won't be considered a threat. I had suggested Buck Sergeant, but the Colonel said an NCO wouldn't be low enough to mingle in the circle we need." Harry and Oliver checked they had their government travel cards current. Harry was directed to get a new ID that showed his assumed rank. They received their orders and headed home to pack. "Come back at 1700 and I'll take you to the Heathrow. By the way Harry, do you mind if I borrow your mini while your away. Mines in the shop. I'd ask Oliver, but his wife needs his. Harry agreed and offered to pick up Oliver on his way back to base.

Back at the office with Oliver in tow, Harry slipped out of the drivers seat and the Captain slid in. "Nice little car this, I'll enjoy tootling around in it." Oliver was going to explain about the starter but when he saw the gleam in Harry's eye decided not to. On the hour and a half drive he explained Oliver's part. Oliver is your point of contact and will keep the base commander filled in on your progress. The base will make the arrest when you have amassed enough evidence. Oliver I suggest you stay in town and come in to base about three times a week. Harry, why don't you two meet at the bowling alley on the days you pick or find another place, it's up to you." On the plane they slept, ate and talked. Oliver silently wondered how the captain was doing starting Harry's car.

Harry had been at Lowry for a week. Oliver was stationed off base at a Howard Johnsons. In Oliver's room they went over what Harry had discovered so far. "There isn't much to report yet, classes are just getting going and the food lab portion won't start till Monday. I've been going to all the recreation places and haven't seen or smelt anything illegal. I think they're careful until they consider the people are comfortable and safe." Oliver considered Harry's report and thought of an idea, "Harry, you might want to start acting stressed out about the course. Your usually confident so they might pass you over as a possible client. If your stressed you might be offered something to calm down. Talk to your instructor about your concerns." Harry considered it a good idea.

The next day he put Oliver's suggestion in action. "TSgt Reynolds, I need to talk to you please." TSgt Reynolds led him into the instructor's office. "What seems to be the problem, Harry?" "Sir, I'm having trouble focusing. I've been working as a SIMS administrator for a while. I guess the stress of trying to remember all the cooking stuff is getting to me." TSgt Reynolds was sympathetic and would see if any of the Training Instructors could give Harry some assistance. Harry thanked TSgt Reynolds and walked out of the office. In class harry displayed all the symptoms of stress. He had a headache, he fidgeted, he even teared up several times. On the hourly ten-minute break TSgt Reynolds approached him. "You really are struggling aren't you." "Yeah, I'm trying hard to focus and I study all night but sometimes I can't remember what the heck I just read. I'm not sleeping at night much so that's not helping either" He rubbed his temple and started to tear up making a show of trying to control himself. TSgt Reynolds promised he'd see if he could get him some help."

The next day TSgt Reynolds approached Harry in the hall. "Look, I've got something that will help you relax enough to get some sleep, Take it tonight a little before you plan on sleeping. Oh, don't tell anyone about this it might prove embarrassing." Harry nodded as if he understood but wasn't quite sure what was meant by embarrassing. He pocketed the pill and spent the rest of the class still putting on a subtle act of nervousness.

Later that evening he went off base to see Oliver. "Good, were making progress," Oliver held the round white tablet and matched it to a picture grid of pills. "looks like you've been given a Quaalude." Harry agreed. "When I was set to leave class today Reynolds asked me what I planned on doing. I told him go back to my room and try and relax. He smiled and told me to take the pill then. I swapped it with an aspirin and took that. After twenty minutes I feigned getting relaxed and slightly sleepy. He escorted me to the dorm and told me to go to bed. Oliver appreciated the way Harry was handling his end. "What's your plan now. "I'll go to class bright eyed and bushy tailed. After two days I'll go back and ask for another. Ten days later I need something to perk me up at which time I should be offered something stronger and highly addicting like cocaine.

Oliver agreed. "Harry, I'm going to swing on base and keep an eye on Reynolds. I want to see who his pharmacist is. Just remember if you see me we don't know each other." Harry saluted and left the room. He was able to get back to his room taking a surreptitious route. There was a note on the door stating he had been called with a return number. He called back and spoke in a lazy sleepy tone. "Harry, sorry to get you up, how are you feeling?" "Sleepy still, I heard someone knocking earlier but couldn't get out of bed." "Yeah, I figured as much so I sent the Dorm guard to check on you, he didn't see you in your room." Harry chuckled into the receiver. "He must not have looked on the window side of the bed against the wall. I had rolled over and was wrapped tight in the sheet and blanket. I was hanging off the side of the bed when I woke up, had a hell of a time unwrapping myself." Reynolds laughed over the line. "Guess that's why he didn't see you, he said he just poked his head in, didn't see you and reported back. I'll make sure he does a thorough check next time. You could have strangled like that." Reynolds hung up still laughing at Harry's predicament. Harry made a mental note to see who was on duty last night and keep an eye on them. If they were working with Reynolds and company, it might make it hard for Harry to see Oliver.

Harry showed up to class looking much better. Reynolds again apologized for waking him and was pleased the "medicine" had helped. On the second of the hourly breaks, he happened to walk to the soda machine and spotted Hattie enjoying a soda of her own. She tossed the can and joined Harry at the machine. He offered to get her a soda which she accepted. He felt a slight pull on his pocket. She took the soda as it emerged and went back to the table.

In a bathroom stall he read the note. "Harry, Oliver called me here to act as his liaison. I'll be here next break, try and pick me up for a stroll after class."

Harry ate the note. His task completed he walked into the Food Lab. It hadn't changed much since he had been here for tech school. New instructors but that was it. The 12 stoves in a rectangle, shelves of pots, pans and utensils. A shelf full of measuring cups and spoons. To the back side was the food locker of spices, and a walk in fridge. Harry was assigned to fill out AF Form 248 for requisitioning the foods they would need for class. He made the pull and chatted with the storeroom person as he waited. He put a supply at each station of what was pulled then took station six. His stove and table was at the rear and center of the room. From there he could see everything and had a wall to his back.

The first part of the class dealt with the recipe card and measurements. On the break Harry went to the soda machine and saw Hattie again. He eyed her speculatively then approached her. She blushed when he asked if he could join her. Over the next ten minutes they talked and found they had many things in common. Harry asked if she wouldn't mind joining him for a walk after school. She looked at him with melting eyes as they made their date. Harry trembled with excitement. He was really playing his part convincingly and so was she.

After class she was waiting at the class door for Harry. They stopped by the dorm so Harry could change and drop off his books. On the stroll Hattie explained why she had been called in. "Oliver was at your dorm asking some questions when Reynolds call came in. He was worried that you two meeting was going to be a problem so he asked if I could come as well. I was on the red eye last evening and arrived early today. He got me a room in the female dorms as a transient. You're lucky to be a senior airman, I have to be an airman first class. She put her arm through his as they walked. A passing security reminded them about no public displays of affection. Hattie took her arm from Harry's, and they continued to walk and talk. They went to the bowling alley and had some pizza for dinner. TSgt Reynolds passed by and when he noticed Harry with Hattie he stopped behind Hattie's line of sight and gave Harry a thumbs up then went to join his league group.

They watched Reynolds bowl for a while and noticed a bag of some sort passing from one of the bowlers to Reynolds. "Looks like marijuana from here." Hattie whispered. Harry nodded. When the person who had passed the bag rose Harry went to the soda dispenser and filled up his cup. He spent some time looking for some packets of parmesan cheese until the man came to replenish his own soda. On his league vest was the name Josh Phillips. Harry returned to his seat and passed the name to Hattie. Dropping Hattie off at the Dorm, Harry went back to his room. He went over the lessons they had for the day and what would be covered tomorrow.

For the next couple of days Harry showed signs of returning stress. By the second day he approached Reynolds again. To Reynolds, Harry appeared nervous and agitated. He was right where Reynolds wanted him. He recognized Harry wanted another Quaalude but was he desperate enough to ask. Harry started to turn away excusing himself then when he turned back and started towards Reynolds again, he knew he had Harry hooked.

"I was wondering if it would be possible to get another of those pills, I'm back where I started and need help. There was a plea in Harry's voice and eyes that pleased Reynolds. "Sure pal, see me after the next break and I'll help you out. Oh, I will need to shell out some money for getting these, it's going to cost you a fiver." Harry face turned glum, but he reached into his pocket for his wallet. "No, not here and now, On the next break come to my office and we'll take care of it then." Harry saw Hattie in the break room and indicated success by buying a Pepsi instead of a Coke.

As Harry and Reynolds performed the swap, the transaction was recorded on a Minox camera through a crack in the door. She hoped she had gotten something usable as she didn't want to be seen hovering by the door and had snapped multiple pictures from the hip as it were. Harry came out and went back to class while Mattie went to the base amateur photo lab and developed the pictures herself. She was lucky that the base had a camera club attached to the Arts and Crafts center. Once the pictures were developed and dried she took them back to her dorm room. Under the lights she checked them with a magnifying glass. She had the picture she needed. It showed Reynolds, the pill and Harry.

The picture was surprisingly detailed and she would be able to enlarge it if needed. She caught a bus for off base and went to make the delivery to Oliver.

For the next week Harry took classes and began to become sluggish and disoriented in class. He had received five more consignments of pills and checked each one carefully. The price went up each time and Harry was concerned they might swap one out to test if he was really taking them. Sure enough one of them was similar but there were marked differences.

One was an asprin. He had tasted the first quaalude and each one. He could tell the difference in look and taste as well as texture. He brought it up to Reynolds who smiled and gave him the correct pill. "Sorry that one didn't do anything for you this should fix you up. How are you doing now?" Harry took the bait. Good, I'm sleeping better at night now and not so jittery. Trouble is I need plenty of coffee to get a jump start in the morning and it isn't helping much. Reynolds had him come into the office.

"Harry, I think I have something that will jump start you just fine." He held out a small plastic bag wrapped at two ends. Inside were five small white crystals. He reached into a pocket of his briefcase and brought out a clear glass tube with some metal a quarter inch from the end. "Put one of those into this at the end here and then just smoke it like you would a cigarette. In fact, you can keep it in a cigarette pack if you need a quick hit. Give it a try and let me know if you need more." Harry thanked him and started to leave.

Reynolds put an arm around Harry's shoulder and led him outside. "Let's do a hit now, you'd be surprised how much you can accomplish with it." Harry was nervous, he had never done drugs before. He was trapped though. The investigation was ongoing and he had to stay in character. He followed Reynolds lead and smoked. He acted as if his heart started racing after a few seconds he acted exalted as if he could do anything. He was filled with energy. He kept rubbing his eyes and looking around.

Reynolds was talking to Harry when Hattie happened around the back of the building. With a hurt look she admonished Harry for missing their meeting in the break room. Reynolds told her to go back inside and that he'd bring Harry up in a couple of minutes. In fact Harry was so far ahead he could take the rest of the day off. Within a few minutes Harry came down. He felt drained and sluggish. "whew! What a rush. It didn't last long though." Harry sounded disappointed which was what Reynolds had been hopping for. "No it doesn't to get through a work day it sometimes takes a few hits to keep going. Then you may want to take a few Q's to ease off at night. Don't worry, I'll keep you covered. Seems like services generally have a problem with being rushed off their feet. A little pick me up helps in the crunch."

He led Harry to where Hattie was waiting and told Harry he was done for the day. Hattie reminded Harry that he had promised her a walk by the river. The river was the water that ran out of one drain pipe, down a slope about fifty yards to another. It ran between the dorms and the commissary. It was also off limits to students. Sitting together Harry described what had just happened. "I was given a small sampling of crack and Reynolds dragged me outside to smoke it. I was able to convince him I was smoking it as he was so wrapped up in smoking his he wasn't paying that close attention. He was just there to make sure I did it and stuck around. Hattie blew out the breath she had been holding. "Harry, you had me scared. I think I'm going to tell Oliver we've got to get you out now. We've got enough evidence on Reynolds and his pharmacist. I think Phillips will be only too eager to give us a list of his clients in exchange for leniency."

Harry lay back and relaxed. "Good, this case is getting to me." Hattie lay back as well and they talked for a little longer. Getting up they saw a security forces cop standing at the Commissary side. Harry started walking towards him. Hattie whispered, "You're crazy, are you *trying* to get in trouble?" Harry whispered back as the space between them and the SP closed. "Nah, if he was going to bust us he'd have been walking our way by now."

He waved and said hello to the SP. "You know that area is off limits to students don't you?" Harry turned wide eyes on the cop. He looked around with a shocked expression, "Gosh no! I didn't see any signs around, sorry sir, we'll keep out from now on." The SP looked them over and hitched his thumb towards the Commissary. If you're going to get some grub better hurry, they close in half an hour." Once inside Hattie had a fit of laughter. "Damn Harry, you keep a cool head in an emergency don't you." Harry smiled and bought some lunchmeat and tortillas.

Oliver sat with a tortilla turkey wrap and went over the case. "We'll pick up Phillips first thing in the morning. Hattie has given me plenty to hang him with. Like you, I think he'll cough up anything we need to save his skin.

Oliver was right and Phillips did indeed hand over all his client records. School was placed on hold and all students were placed on Dorm restrictions. All except Harry and Hattie who was on a golden eagle flight back to Mildenhall leaving Oliver to complete the case. At Heathrow the captain was there to pick them up and all the way to Mildenhall complained about having to push start Harry's damn mini every time he needed to go somewhere.

TEAM SPIRIT

OSI agents Oliver, Harry, and Rudy stepped off the C130 with the rest of the two hundred and fifty troops that were representatives of Services squadrons from all over. Waiting for the buses on the tarmac they discovered that Korea at this time of the year was cold and wet. Harry pulled the hood over his poncho and stomped his feet to get warm. They were here for part of an exercise called Team Spirit. Services were there to build a deployment base from scratch.

South Korea was known to be party central in certain areas, so it promised to be an interesting deployment. Everyone boarded the buses to go to the bare bones site in Pusan. The bus pulled into a large section that was gated off and full of mud, rocks and small patches of grass. It was barren except for large green wooden chests strewn all over. These contained the tents they would live in for the duration of their stay as well as being used for offices and kitchen/dining area.

It was a case of hit the ground running and the OSI team spent the next few hours setting up their tent and office. For this exercise three agents had been sent. Oliver, Harry and Rudy, Rudy was from Scott Air Force Base while Harry and Oliver were from Mildenhall U.K. Rudy was a cocksure new troop who was dead sure he knew everything, "The newbie's always do." Oliver responded to Harry pointing this out. As senior member he was in charge of his small group.

They divided the tent. Back half for sleeping and the front as their office. Harry opened up the case that held their desk and files. While Oliver went to the Command post to check them in. It amused Harry to set the desk up. The case the desk and was part shelving unit the desk was a piece of plastic fit into a slot with legs that folded down. The file cabinet was half of the other part of the case and was rolled out and the chairs setup. Harry loved the simplicity and design of the desk. Rudy was unimpressed by the field desk and was anxious to find out what their task would be

Oliver returned with an interesting assignment. They were to go into town to T Street and look over the whore houses and determine which should be placed off limits. Oliver was apologetic as he read the note, "I know this is a disappointment for you guys, but we can't turn down a job just because it's dirty." Harry grimaced at Rudy's excitement, they changed into comfortable clothes and jumped onto the bus for town.

Doing a walk up and down T Street was not much entertainment when you're doing an inspection. Most of the places had certifications of the bar girls ensuring they were free of STD's. The ones that didn't were marked as off limits. Rudy was disappointed they weren't going to *inspect* further but Oliver promised Rudy he'd have plenty of time to do his own "inspection" later.

They stopped at a place called Fools Rush In for a quick meal. Harry ordered rice, Doenjang Jjigae (a type of stew) and Kimchi. Oliver settled for Rice and Budae Jjigae (Korean Army Stew). Rudy just wanted a Pajeon or Korean Pancake. This place had females who acted as companions but were not the type who you, well you know. Harry and Oliver bought some lunch for the girls while Rudy sat at a separate table and bought his companion drinks. When he ran out of money, he approached Harry for a loan. "I just need twenty bucks for more drinks, she really likes me!" Harry refused to make a loan stating, "Rudy, if she really liked you, you wouldn't need the twenty."

After lunch they went back to camp and helped putting up the kitchen tent and walked around aiding wherever they could. They're part of the exercise was information gathering and analysis that wouldn't start until tomorrow. In the meantime Rudy went back off base with a promise to be back in a couple of hours. Harry and Oliver went over plans for the next day and night. Duty shifts at night would be slow so they placed Rudy on that. "It's a little unfair to stick the new guy on nights don't you think? Harry asked.

Oliver called out, "Hey Rudy, you against taking the night shift?" He waited for a response, "Doesn't seem to care one way or the other," and made the rest of the schedule up. When three o'clock rolled around and Rudy hadn't returned Oliver was perturbed. "He's probably doing a close-up inspection at one of the pleasure palaces. Harry, I have to attend a table top at the CC in half an hour. Go downtown, locate him and haul his ass back here." Harry shrugged into a jacket and hopped on the bus. All the way into town he worked out how the hell he was supposed to find Rudy short of knocking on every door.

The bus let him off at the market that was selling all sort of cheap souvenirs to the gullible tourists. Harry skirted around the stalls and followed the river the three blocks to T Street. The restaurant they had eaten at earlier was still open. It was at the entrance to T Street and from there you could see everything. Being a closed street made it convenient for searching. All up and down were Kiosks where you could change money. Harry approached each and asked about a friend of his. Up one side and down the next he found the right one near the beginning opposite the first he had tried.

"I remember him, he changed two hundred dollars. He's going to have a big time!" The man said with a grin. Something in the man's eye caught Harry's attention. There was more than laughter there. Without turning his head Harry looked to the side and saw the money changers eyes were cast towards a Jeepney. These little motorized trikes were everywhere ferrying passengers all over. A tap on his back made him swing around. The young lady who had tapped him jumped back quickly. Harry had a good memory for faces and hers was one he wouldn't forget. She had been Rudy's companion earlier.

"Buy me a drink?" She said it differently than he had heard it earlier. There was urgency in her voice that ensured his attention. He took her into Fools Rush In and bought them both a drink. He was amused to notice that his was a normal scotch and soda while hers was colored water. She sat close to him and practically whispered in his ear. "I saw your friend when he came back, when he changed a lot of money the light on top of the changing booth changed to flashing."

Harry could guess the rest. An offer to take him to a place off the street where the girls were better was a good inducement to trap Rudy. "Can you give me an idea of what direction they went?" She drew a map on a napkin. She added some identifiers if the Jeepney so if it was still outside the spot he'd recognize it. Harry reached into his back pocket to tip her but she staid his hand. "No, he was a nice person and I just want to make sure he's okey."

Harry recognized that she was a good person in a bad position. He thanked her for the information and found a driver he felt he could trust. There wasn't much to go on, so he had to go with his gut. He gave directions from the map he held. It took him part ways then he had to eyeball trying to find the jeepney she had described. They were doing a circuit going wider each time. In ten minutes Harry spied the Jeepney.

Harry paid the man with a generous tip. "I'll wait," Said the driver, "If you're not out in fifteen minutes, I'll come in." Harry grinned, He had guessed right and this guy had his back. A surripticious glance through a tear in a drawn blind showed Rudy playing cards. From the glance he saw that Rudy had a small stack of chips and the other man's was very large. Rudy had been losing steadily.

Harry understood the situation. Rudy had been inveigled into taking the taxi, brought to this location and then induced to play cards whereby he would be stripped of his money in such a way that it wasn't exactly theft. Rudy's face was dripping sweat, with his money almost gone he wasn't sure what would happen next. Would they try and find more, hold him for ransom, or worse. Harry knocked and when his knock was unanswered he tried the door. Locked as he had expected but with a lock that was no security. Working quietly with a thin metal card he had the door open in moments.

A forceful shove and he rolled into the room and stood upright in a corner. The man at the door whipped out a knife but the man at the table raised his hand and the knife was sheathed. The man at the table indicated a chair, Harry shook his head no. "I am sure my friend here has enjoyed his game of poker but I'm afraid he must be leaving." The man at the door locked it more securely. Rudy was still scared but with backup he regained a little of his composure.

The man at the doorway was standing with his arms crossed leaning back. Harry could see the gleam of brass knuckles and understood. Reaching into his pocket he wrapped his fingers around a roll of quarters. The added weight meant a more devastating punch. Rudy might have been inexperienced but wasn't stupid, just naïve. He backed into a corner as well. Harry looked relaxed as he kept both men in his line of vision. "Gentlemen, we have enjoyed your company but must take our leave, how we go about this is in your hands." The man at the door straightened and the man behind the table pushed it aside.

There was no doubt how this was going to go down. The man at the door was tall and muscular but slow, the man at the table was faster but unarmed. The tall man lunged and swung for Harry's face. Harry had been expecting that and wheeled out of harms way. He brought a weighted fist down on the outstretched arm. Grasping the man by the neck he threw him to the corner he had vacated. Rudy was going for the straight attack and kicked at the man's knees and punched at the throat. It was a surprisingly quiet fight with grunts and the sound of well-aimed punches. Rudy may not have been a seasoned fighter but he had good training. He had his man down and tied with his own belt. Harry went for another swift strike wheeling to increased the force of the punch and his man went down.

The floor was littered with quarters as the wrapping broke with the force of Harry's thrust. Harry opened the door and the Jeepney driver waived them inside. He sped away bringing them eventually to the border of T Street. All the way he spoke to Rudy about the dangers of changing large amounts of money at a single changer. "You do a little at few of them, take your time and don't do it all at once." He gave a lecture Rudy wouldn't forget. When they arrived safe Harry paid again and bought their driver dinner.

On the bus Rudy apologized for letting his enthusiasm get the better of him. "You're new to the game and weren't paying attention to the briefing." He grinned at Rudy. Poor kid his first experience of Korea was to be shanghaied and to lose a couple of weeks wages in the process. Back on base Rudy was instructed as to their mission and working conditions. He was going to complain about working the night shift but a look at Harry and he decided that night shift was just the shift he wanted. That evening Rudy held the fort while Harry and Oliver did some sightseeing.

Walking along the river they bought some food from the street vendors. The pancakes filled with vegetables were very good and a side of kimchi was the perfect accompaniment. Desiring something for dessert they approached a vender who was selling something that looked like fish shaped doughnuts. Harry shrugged off the unusual shape but Oliver decided to wait and see how Harry enjoyed it first. Harry said it smelt alright and promptly took a large bite. That bite had contained fried batter and inside a large collection of fish eggs. Harry immediately dropped it and spat out the rest. Oliver was laughing at the startled look on Harry's face.

Wandering around the stalls and few shops they picked up a mink blanket each and Harry bought Maddie a robe with a dragon embroidered on the back. Oliver was entranced by a cheep plastic pocket watch that was also a lighter. Arriving back to base they checked in with Rudy and went to bed. Tomorrow promised to be a busy day.

A SHIRT'S DILEMA

First Sergeant Talbot was standing outside his last no notice room inspection. So far it had tried his patience as room after room failed. He had to call in a couple of other first shirts to talk to their people. As the Services First Shirt the dorms were under his jurisdiction and this was one of his duties. It always surprised him that the female rooms were pretty consistently dirtier than the men's. He knocked even though he knew the occupant was away on leave for the next couple of days, but it was part of the procedure. He opened the door first calling out "First Sergeant". As the door opened he was relieved that before Airman Carter went on leave he had done a good job on his room.

Senior Master Sergeant Talbot admired the shined boots lined up under the bed, The books neat and tidy on the bookcase, Clothes in the locker were pressed and folded neatly. He raised the cover on the desk and received a shock as all under here was chaos. He poked around a but and looked through a small selection of photos. There were several that he recognized as pictures of Mildenhall. Under these were five pictures of the desk. He compared it with the desks current condition. They were pretty much similar. When he had gone through First Sergeant training they had impressed upon him the importance of the unusual. The instructor had been emphatic that what was unusual was usually important. If people took pictures of something then it was to record something important to them, he brought the pictures to the window. Looking at them from every angle he couldn't make out any reason to have taken the picture let alone five of them. He was concerned enough to take them to OSI to have their analyst look over them.

OSI Agent Hattie Martin was glad to have something to analyze It had been a slow morning and she was going off her rocker with boredom. She was wearing a magnifying headpiece and scanning the picture under a bright light. Harry came up for a chat but seeing she was engaged quietly seated himself and placed her coffee nearby. Eventually Hattie took off the magnifiers and rubbed her eyes. When she saw Harry and the coffee she brightened up a bit. "What are you working on?" Harry asked as he passed some sugar packets over. Ripping open four she stirred them into her coffee and then drank it off in one gulp. With her free hand she passed over the picture and magnifier. "Damned if I know what I'm supposed to be looking at. It's just some airman's desk but they think there might be more to it than that, take a look and tell me what you see." Harry placed the magnifier on his head and looked at the picture, "Bags of crisps, 2 sodas, a yorkie bar, a mechanical Uncle Sam bank, his CDC's and notes. The rest is just some various trash." He took the picture and looked at it under the light. "I see a cigar, and a pipe, pipe tobacco, reamer and tamp. Those are all at the back so he must not smoke often. I really don't see anything illicit."

Harry called over Oliver and had him look. As Oliver perused the picture and compared it with the others he wrote out his findings adding his notes to Hattie's and Harry's. I see some gum stuck under the top of the desk by the light, marks from when he was using the desk to shine his shoes and boots. A can of polish sideways and tucked at the right rear with a folded yellow shine cloth above." Squinting through the lenses he tried to see anything Hattie and Harry hadn't found. He handed the picture back and removed the magnifier. He shrugged and went back to his desk. Harry stayed a little longer to visit but then had to get back to his own work. Hattie took the list that the three of them had made and filled out her report to give to the First Sergeant.

My other mysteries

ROCKY REPORTER GETS HIS FIRST SCOOP

"Hey Rocky, get your recorder and camera and head out to the old jail on Newark street. They're closing it down and moving the dead. See what you can dig up on it. Check with the folks who turn up. You might be able to get a personal angle from a few." The Chief leaned out of his office. He watched with approval as Rocky Stone, new reporter for the Logan Sentinel leapt from his desk banging his knee in the process, grabbed his recorder and a camera, checked there was a tape in the recorder and film in the camera then headed out. At the door he pulled on his navy coat and his old Greek fisherman's cap off the peg and placed it at a jaunty angle.

Editor in Chief Nelson went back into his office and looked over the list of events for today and marked off who would cover what. Taking a pull at his pipe, he patted himself on the back for hiring Rocky at such short notice. A good kid fresh out of the army where he had been a journalist. Once his two years were up, he had come back home looking for work and had been accepted immediately. Nelson felt sure that with time Rocky would become his star reporter. He had energy, industry and was the friendly sort who people felt comfortable talking to.

Stepping into the street Rocky breathed deeply of the crisp morning air. The jail wasn't far and the day pleasant, he decided to walk. It was two blocks down Quincy Street, turn right onto Jarvis Avenue and another two blocks down then left onto Haskins past an open expanse of brown grass and boulders and there it was. An imposing edifice that still gave him the chills every time he drove past it. He approached the building with a sense of disquiet.

He walked up to the chain link fence that bordered the property. The fence had concertina wire on the top and was buried three feet down into the ground at the bottom. Through the chain link fence, he saw another about three feet from this one. He brought out his camera and snapped a couple of pictures showing a group of people standing around as workmen dug down into the graves and pulled out the caskets. Some had to be wrapped in plastic first then laid in a sling to be raised. Once on the surface the plastic was cut and the remains or what remained of the remains were transferred to a new coffin, the name of the individual written on a card and the card tacked to the top of the casket. Finally, the casket would be loaded onto a flatbed for transport to the plot of land designated for reburial. He wasn't a hardened reporter yet and the sight made him slightly nauseous. As usual he called on his sense of humor to relax him.

Rocky pulled up the collar of his navy pea coat up and tapped the cop at the gate on the shoulder. Officer Woodward turned around and frowned when he came face to face with a man in a Pea Coat, Upside down Greek Fisherman's cap, eyes crossed, a cigarette in his ear and smoke coming out of his nose. "Rocky, you have got to be the craziest reporter at the Sentinel." Rocky retrieved the cigarette and took a drag. "I've got to cover the move, mind if I slide inside?" Officer Woodward opened the gate and let him pass inside.

Rocky snapped a few pics of the building and another long shot of the bodies raising from the pit. As he edged closer to the cemetery he turned to take a shot of a window. Behind that frosted glass he recognized where the death room was. He stood and stared as images of hangings and electrocutions flashed through his mind. One in particular recurred over and over. A man, slight of build and with a shock of red hair being led into the chair. A priest mumbles a prayer that is barely audible. If it is meant to comfort the condemned its purpose is lost on the young man in the chair. In his mind's eye he could smell the burning flesh and hear the crackle of electricity. The young man's body contorts in the chair as the current pours through him. He slumps and is carried away. he sees a young wife nearby her eyes red with tears and a boy of four years old clinging to her skirt. His eyes are red also but there is firmness in his stance and purpose in his stare. The image has been burned into his memory to be carried with him the rest of his life.

A tap on his shoulder brought him out of his reverie. He turned to look upon a man with red hair and a red beard and mustache. He was tall and slightly built, his mouth was usually held in grim lines, but his smile was pleasant as he too looked up at the frosted pane. "I saw you looking up there and wondered what held your interest so long." Rocky shook the images from his mind. "It's the death house, I saw it in my mind. I saw flashes of people going to their death." The man took a pull at his pipe and then looked from the window to the graveyard. "I been there and saw it for myself. I'm here to watch them move my dad to his new home." He turned and walked to a grave that they were just starting to open. Rocky joined him. "I'm a reporter for the Settler, mind talking with me a bit." The red headed man looked at Rocky and seemed as though he was trying to take the measure of him. "Guess so, I don't know that anyone would want to hear what I got to say though." Rocky brought out his recorder and double checked the tape.

"You said no one would want to hear what you have to say, well I do." The man leaned against a post and his eyes took on a mile long stare. "This is where my dad is buried. He had just turned twenty five and his birthday was spent on death row. Me and my mom were brought in to see him die in the chair. I can still hear my dad calling to me, "Son, I swear I'm innocent don't you ever doubt that." I never did, they said he killed a woman and buried her out in a field. My dad and I used to go to that self same field and bring our dog to chase sticks. There was a clump of trees that hid a small grassy area. One day our dog chased the ball into it and started howling and scratching at a pile of freshly dug earth there. Dad didn't like the way Russ was barking so he had me stand behind a big oak to wait while he and Russ checked it out. They scraped away together till they uncovered a woman. I went over to the tree that was on the edge of the small plot. I was peeking from around the tree and saw her when Dad rolled her over. Her head was caved in on the right as though she'd been hit with a bat or something. She couldn't have been dead long because the blood was still fresh. It got onto Dads arm and hand. I saw the sheriff's car drive up and the deputy turned on his lights and pulled his gun on Dad. Dad got up slowly motioning me to stay put. Russ was growling at the deputy and the deputy shot him. Dad had his hands out in front of him and next thing I knew Dad was on the ground on his face and the deputy was cuffing him and half dragging him into the squad car." He pulled a handkerchief out of a back pocket and mopped his brow.

"I ran home and had to wait until my mom got home. When she came in, I was still crying but eventually got out that dad had been taken to jail." He paused as he heard the chunk of metal on wood. "The trial was so short it couldn't even be called a trial. We couldn't afford a lawyer and the one they gave dad wasn't any good. It was over before we knew it and the look on my dad's face was one we'll never forget. He was set to go to the chair on the 23rd of March, his birthday. The deputy came and got us to go see it. I sat in the same car, on the same side, looked out the same window dad had. They took us up to the second floor and we stood at the side behind a guardrail. Like I said, I knew my dad was innocent, He wouldn't hurt anybody cept to protect us. No one ever listened. We've been trying for years to clear his name. I still am trying to clear it. I can't say I've gotten any closer after all these years."

He stood as the casket came out of the earth. Rocky recognized that there wasn't much wrong with the casket. It had to be one of the last to be laid in. The casket was labeled and placed on the end and edge of the flatbed. "See you soon dad" the man said as he touched the wood. Pulling a dark green Greek Fisherman's hat out of a pocket he placed it on his head. He was walking away when he turned and hollered for Rocky. "Hey mister, Why don't you come with me, mom and me will give you dinner. Price is right and you won't find better." Rocky held up a hand indicating he'd be with him in a moment. He'd found his story and wasn't going to let it slip away.

Rocky finished off his roll of film and joined his new companion. As they passed Officer Woodward, they heard him laughing. Both turned at the sound. "Sorry fellas but you too could pass as family!" It was only then they realized the similarity in their coat and hat. Both were of similar height and weight. Rocky extended his hand. "The names Rocky Stone, pleased to make your acquaintance. His new friend reached out and grasped Rocky's hand in a firm grip, "Mine's Joe Steckler, Nice to meet you."

They walked down Leeward Street for a few blocks chatting casually as if they were already old friends. At the corner of Leeward and Windward Joe led them up the steps onto the porch of a small home. Joe opened the door shouting that he had company. From inside Rocky heard the clatter of heels over wood. Mrs Steckler opened the door wide in a welcoming gesture. Joe led Rocky into a fairly spartan living room with an old couch and a couple of metal folding chairs in front of a wood table that looked as if it had been made out of wood crates. A Crosley radio stood on the top shelf of the bookcase playing Benny Goodman softly in the background. On a shelf was a newly framed diploma. Joe had just graduated from High School and from the look of the ornate frame his mother was very proud of him.

Rocky was seated on the dilapidated couch and Joe sat on one of the chairs. Mrs. Steckler brought in coffee and cake and sat them on the table. Looking at Rocky she gradually seemed to relax. Joe leaned back in his chair with his coffee cupped in his hands. "Ma, I've been telling Rocky here about Dad and that we've been trying for years to clear his name. He thinks he might be able to help us." Rock held up his hand. "I said I'm willing to look into it and do some research. With the access I have I might be able to stir up something. I just don't want you to pin all your hopes on me." Mrs. Steckler seemed to grow smaller than her five foot three inches as she huddled miserably in her chair. Rocky stood behind her and put his hand on her shoulder. Squatting beside her chair he looked into her eyes. "Sorry, I didn't mean that to sound harsh but it might take a while to get what we need, but we'll get it. I'll work on this as much as possible and when were really ready, ready with proof we'll break this story wide open. We might even be able to find the real murderer." Mrs. Steckler laid a hand on his shoulder and leaning on it as she raised herself and walked unsteadily into the kitchen to put the finishing touches to dinner.

"It might help to see what you've done so far, that way I can fill in what blanks are missing." Rocky sat back down as Joe reached under the couch for a long thin dress box. From inside he pulled a couple of old, yellowed newspapers, a transcript of the trial and the Death certificate. Rocky leaned back into the couch and read of what was printed about Joes father while Joe headed out to set the table.

June 15th, 1928 - local sheriff's deputy Warren Lester apprehended Mr. Joseph P Steckler. Mr. Steckler is accused of the Murder of Ms. Laura Holmes 22. She was reported missing by her mother at 1430 on the June 13th after not returning from a morning walk.

June 16th, 1928 - Mr. Joseph P Steckler has been remanded for trial on June 20th. His Court appointed Lawyer has already announced that they will be pleading innocent and that there is no proof as to the guilt of his client. He is concerned with the speed with which the prosecutor is driving this trial at the insistence of the sheriff's office under the direction of Deputy Warren Lester, Sheriff Morgan is still in New Falls on extended duty. Deputy Lester has been unavailable for interview but has issued the following statement. "Mr. Steckler was apprehended in the act of digging a hole preparatory for burying the corpus. Ms. Holmes was only recently dead as the blood was still seeping from the head wound. From these facts we have no doubt as to the verdict of the jurors."

June 20th, 1928 – The trial of Mr. Joseph P Steckler was widely attended today, and the hall was filled to capacity. The prosecutions only witness was Deputy Lester. Deputy Lester was performing his drive around town when he approached Soldier Field and saw the accused after having dug a hole in the process of burying the body of Ms. Holmes. Ms. Holmes had been a close acquaintance of the Deputy and he broke down in tears when he described the finding of her body. He quickly recovered himself and gave the rest of his evidence with a firm voice. Mr. Steckler took the stand and spoke on having brought his dog to the field and while there the dog started digging in the earth and whining. Mr. Steckler had assisted in digging and discovered the body buried in the shallow grave. He had pulled the body out and had laid it on the ground when Deputy Lester had driven by.

Deputy Lester had immediately placed him in custody and charged him with the murder of Ms. Holmes. Upon cross examination as to why, once he had discovered the body he had not immediately contacted the sheriff's office instead of disturbing the scene he answered that since there was still blood seeping from the wound it might be possible to revive her. Dr. Mortimer was called next and gave it as his opinion that the deceased had been dead between 10 to 20 minutes and that death was caused by blunt force trauma to the cranium. The jury deliberated for half an hour and rendered a verdict of guilty. Judge Splicer agreed with the verdict and Mr. Steckler was sentenced to death by electric chair on the 23rd.

Rocky put down the papers and looked up as Joe reentered the room. "Seems to me that the trial was rushed through pretty quick." Joe nodded, "Yeah that's what we think. I somehow think the Deputy had something to do with it but can't prove it. He just seemed to be too johnny on the spot somehow. Besides he knew her and mighta had a falling out with her and resented it." Rocky drank off his cup off cold coffee and was ushered into the dining room. Over a dinner of homemade noodles and beef shank they started working out a plan of attack. Rocky made a list of the people involved and who knew who as well as the facts or what was considered facts. The town of Comfort Ohio was a small one and he felt with time and patience he might be able to uncover some new ground. Leaning back in his chair he complimented Mrs. Steckler on dinner. She smiled at him, "We don't have a lot but make do and we get by." Joe patted his mother's shoulder on his way to the kitchen with a stack of bowls. "Mom could make a carboard box into a feast and you'd never notice it was cardboard."

Rocky ticked off his notes and asked about some of the people on his list. "Did you know Ms. Holmes?" Her face frowned and he could see the muscles of her wrist tighten as she clenched the arm of the chair. "I knew of her, everyone knew of her. She was a little flirt is what she was, if it wore slacks she'd bat her eyes and swivel her hips at em." Rocky was surprised at the vehemence as she spat out her words. "She was stringing along Deputy Lester but that didn't mean she was his exclusive. She had plenty of fish on a hook and it weren't any secret who she kept dangling." Rocky made a note then asked about the Deputy. "He was alright as far as being a deputy goes. A little to zealous if you ask me and to cock sure of himself when Sheriff Morgan was off somewhere. I think the shock of seeing Shirley dead in front of Joe was what made him treat Joe so bad and made him push the trial up quick.

Rocky spent a while more with them then politely took his leave. Joe saw him to the door. "Don't think to much about what ma said, she never liked Sue Holmes. She felt that sooner or later she'd hit on Pa. Dad wouldn't of gone with her though and she knows it. She just didn't like that kind of fast woman." The men shook hands and Rocky sauntered down the street. He had a few more hours of work ahead of him so he went back to the Settler to talk over the story with his boss.

"I think there might be a story in this somewhere. I'll write up about the closing of the Jail but I'd like to give this a little play. Should tug at the heartstrings a bit. A Man wrongly placed on death row for a murder he didn't commit. Family destitute. Son having a hard time getting work as the son of a murderer. What do you say?" Nelson leaned back in his chair, his hands behind his head. "I don't see why not. I'll give you a couple of weeks to work on this exclusive. If after two weeks you don't have anything you'll have to give it up and get back to work on regular stories. Deal?" Rocky stood and clasped his boss's hand. "Deal! Bet you a steak dinner that I either prove his guilt or find who did it!" Nelson shook his head, "make it a catfish fry and you got a bet."

As Rocky sat at his desk to type out his story about the jail move, he devoted a portion of his mind to the task he had agreed to. First thing after I finish this story I need to get as much as the Settler has about this, then talk to Sheriff Lester. I better tread carefully with him. Why was Mrs. S so pissed about Sue. Neither of them said anything about Joseph being seduced by her. Maybe she just didn't like fast women and feared he could have been tempted.

He finished up his story, placed the roll of film into a canister and added it to the envelope and placed it in the tray. He made his way to the back copies and got out the ones from the trial and everything related to it. In one he found a picture of Sue Holmes. She was attractive in a Gloria Grahame sort of way. She had a kind of dreamy film star look about her and he could understand how men would be attracted. From what the pages said she was a well known personage who hung around the theater and bars. He could imagine she never had to buy her own drinks much. He reread the notes of the trial and studied the picture and side notes Nathen had made while covering the story.

During the trial Joseph Steckler had remained subdued answering questions in a quiet though clear voice. He consistently claimed to having found the body and was upset that the Deputy had shot his dog. The deputy was very vocal and his testimony was very damaging to the defense. He found the defendant beside an open hole with the body still bleeding in his arms. The defendant had a vicious dog as a guardian and he had to shoot it in self-defense. Yes, he had known the victim and was in fact engaged to her. No that would not have made him unnaturally emotional. He had been in firm control the entire time and performed his duty with calmness and efficiency. The defense tried to bring the Deputies performance records in but the prosecutor objected and the judge agreed they had no bearing on the facts of the case. When asked how he had gotten to the site so quickly without being summoned he had stated he was out on patrol. When it was pointed out that the field where the body had been found was in another counties jurisdiction he responded that the area was border and could rightfully be claimed by either. A thought struck him. He rechecked everything. Where was the Sheriff's comments and opinions? There was nothing here and surly something of this magnitude would have been enough to bring the Sheriff back home. He grabbed a notebook and headed over to the sheriff's house.

Stopping outside the sheriff's home he gave his hair a quick comb and pat down. Sheriff Morgan was held in such regard by the community that he was still called Sheriff even though he had retired years ago in fact he still retained the authority if he ever wanted to use it. The door was opened to his knock by his daughter Agnes. She was a young attractive woman about his own age. He had seen her about town once in a while, even being fortunate to having had lunch several times with her. She welcomed him in as a friend. "If you've come to see dad he'll be down in a bit. If he was still working last night would have been his night duty so, he was up all night and in bed at 0500.

Sheriff Morgan came down the stairs stretching and yawning. He started when he saw Rocky sitting with a cup of coffee and a half eaten biscuit. Agnes came back in with the pot and placed it on the coffee table. Kissing her father she told him to sit and she'd bring in some more biscuits and jam. Rocky placed his cup and plate on the table, rose and shook the Sheriffs outstretched hand. "You're the newest reporter for the Herald aren't you?" Rocky nodded and retrieved his cup.

"Yes sir, I'm doing some research on the Sue Holmes case. I was wondering if I could ask you some questions." The sheriff refilled his cup and lay back in his chair. Stretching his legs onto an ottoman he shrugged. "Fire away but if you've done any investigating at all you know I wasn't here at the time." Rocky nodded acknowledging that he already knew that. "It's more in the nature of getting your opinion of some of the people involved I'm interested in.

Rocky pulled out his notebook and recorder. Placing the recorder on the table he started his inquiry. "Let's take Sheriff Lester first." Morgan put his feet on the floor and leaned forward in his chair. "He was a damn decent deputy, a bit overzealous at times and usually taking things at the letter of the law but he was fair. It wasn't very often that I had to overrule an arrest of his. He was a good deputy and he's making a good name for himself as sheriff now." Rocky made a note, Defensive of deputy, doesn't want to hear a word against him. "How about Sue Holmes?" Morgan's posture relaxed again as he replaced his feet on the ottoman and lit a cigarette. "She was an alright kid, just high spirited. I know Lester fell pretty hard for her and expected her to be his girl alone, she couldn't be tied down though. I was surprised when he said she and he were engaged." Rocky checked off an item on his list of questions. "The deputy was on the spot pretty quick, was that area a regular route for you both." Sheriff Morgan rubbed his chin. "Not too often, but it was on one of our routes and if we had stopped off at the Hot Dog Hut for a bite we'd head over that way and eat. Nice view over there with the field trees and river running through." "Was Lester popular around town." Sheriff Morgan snickered, "Mostly with the ladies, he's a good lookin feller and even some of the married ladies took a shine to him." "Didn't that make some of the husbands and boyfriends jealous?" Morgan shook his head. "They may have carried a torch for him, but he never lit 'em."

Rocky didn't feel this line of questioning was getting him anywhere. He sat back and tried to think of anything that might give him a lead. "Sheriff, I'm going to ask you a blunt question, do you think there might have been a mistake made and that the man they electrocuted might have been innocent. The trial was real quick and it seemed the Judge and Deputy Lester were pretty tight." That seemed to strike a nerve and he could see Morgan cloud up for a storm. "The reason the trial went quick was the overwhelming evidence, He was found with the fresh body in his lap ready to bury it. There wasn't any doubt about it." "Just out of curiosity has Lester ever kept an eye out on the Stecklers?" Morgan Lay back in his chair and seemed to be going back to sleep. "I hear tell he has checked on them once in a while. There wasn't much he could do for them, poor folks. Seems they had inherited the house and never owned a car. Mrs Steckler does odd jobs to keep food on the table and seems to make enough for what they need. I expect now her boy is done with school that He'll take care of her now." Rocky thanked the Sheriff for his time and was led to the door by Agnes. "Good luck with your story but I really don't think you'll get much new." She smiled on him with a mixture of encouragement and pity.

Since it was now close to lunch time, he headed over to the Hot Dog Hut and got some lunch. He sat at a table at the back and watched as people came in and went. The place had a steady stream of customers, and the servers were kept hopping.

Several called out in greeting as Sherriff Lester walked in. He greeted them as a celebrity would have. His order must have been consistent because he was served without having to order. He was also served without having to pay. Lester looked around for a place to sit. He saw Rocky pouring over his notes and joined him.

Rocky looked up just as the remains of a smirk were wiped off of the Sheriffs face. What replaced it was a smug grin. Rocky closed his notebook and concentrated on his hotdog. "So, how's the ace reporter from the Sentinel finding things out in the sticks. Heard you came back from the Army to this backwater town." Rocky finished off his first dog and raised the second. "You forget I was born here. My place is down on Sycamore Street. After being out in the middle of nowhere for a couple of years coming back here was a big deal to me." Lester regarded him stoically for a moment. "I hear your trying to make a name for yourself by digging up one of my old cases." His voice came out in a menacing grumble that made Rocky pause. He put down his hotdog and placed his arms on the table. He leaned slightly forward and looked the sheriff square in the eyes. "I was doing a interview about the jails closing. I met a kid there who was looking after his fathers move. We had some dinner and I said I'd see if I could find anything new. So far there doesn't seem to be anything new to find." He shrugged his shoulders and finished his hotdog. Sheriff Lester looked Rocky over then relaxed a little. He gulped down his dog in two bites and slurped his soda. "You won't find anything else cause there isn't anything new to find. Poke around all you want, the trails cold and gone." Rocky made a mental note how the Sheriff seemed to relax once he had stated that he couldn't find anything new. To Rocky that meant that there probably was something to find.

Rocky thought about his current location and that the field where the body was found was nearby. Perhaps a survey of the ground might elicit something or at least give him some feeling to go on. So far he had found very little, to wit nothing. . Rocky headed over to the field checking his camera enroute. A portion had been converted to a cemetery and now was the (hopefully) final resting place from the jails deceased. Up the road strode Joe carrying a metal detector. The smoke from his pipe looking like the puffs from a steam engine. Rocky hailed him as he approached the gate. "Checking to see if your pop stayed put?" Joe patted the detector and untied a satchel from his waist. Laying the detector on the ground he pulled out a selection of objects. "I come here and do a little hunting once in a while. I've found all sorts of things including some civil war objects. Today I thought I'd try the grove over here and see what I can find, come on, lets see what we get."

Rocky followed where Joe led. He had never done any detecting of this sort and was curious how deep things could be found. "Well I rarely go deeper then maybe a foot or so." He pulled out a shovel from the satchel and attached it to his belt. It was collapsible and convenient to carry. "Best part is it even has a compass and a knife in the handle. I love things that serve more than one purpose." Rocky sat on a log and watched Joe work. He was covering the ground in wide sweeps moving slowly forward. After about twenty steps he marked the area and began to dig. He found something and washed it off with water from his canteen. "A bottle cap." He flicked it away and filled in the hole again. Approaching a clump of trees growing tightly together he slid the detector inside and did a quick search. "I don't expect to find," his words were cut off as a squelch emitted from his headset. "Odd, wouldn't have expected anything in this area. I was just being thorough." He half lay over a root and dug. Rocky was curious and hovered over his shoulder. Joe pulled out an oblong piece of metal and attached to some cloth. "Cool, looks like I might have found a medal!" He washed it off disclosing a broach and a flowered piece of material. Joe handed it to Rocky. On the back he scrapped mud away showing faded initials he couldn't make out. "Take a look at the cloth. Seems to be a stain on it."

Joe looked at it carefully. "No way of knowing what it is." Rocky asked to see it again. "I can send it in to a lab we use. Probably apple butter or coffee." Joe nodded and Rocky wrapped it up in paper then placed it into an envelope. "I'll get the chief to send it out on the QT. I've got a feeling it won't be ketchup on this. Might even have belonged to the lady who was killed here." Joe stood up and regained his detector for some more detecting. He waived to Rocky as he left to post off the broach. An idea was forming in the back of Rocky's mind that he didn't like.

"Chief, can we post this to the lab. I want to know what the stain is." His editor scrutinized the broach then wrapped and packaged it in a small box. "Better take it there and wait for the result." He wrote down the address and handed it over. "I'll call Phill and let him know your coming." "Thanks Chief, if it's what I think it is I may come back to see you about how to handle it." Nelson cocked an eyebrow at Rocky's retreating back. Rocky had been keeping him up to date on his investigation and it was the first time he had anything definite, well almost definite. This kid was tenacious and if there was anything in this story, he felt sure Rocky could find it.

At the Lab Phil took the package and carefully removed the paper. Putting it through the test he pulled the results from the analyzer. "O.k. the initial finding is blood and it is human. It's type O positive so as there aren't schools of people with it, the Sheriff should be able to narrow it down. He sat down on the edge of his desk and folded his arms over his chest. "Rocky, Phil gave me a little information regarding this. He called in a favor I owed him and I am not going to say anything. However, if this is what you both think it is I can come out with the information whenever you want it.

Back in the Sentinal Rocky brought out a set of magnifying glasses. He scraped a pencil and wetting his finger rubbed the lead into the back of the broach. The initials L.H., odds were good it belonged to the murdered woman. So, now what. Rocky took a picture of the broach and made some notes. He made his way home for dinner and stopped off at the Stickler's to see Joe on the way. Mrs. Steckler opened the door at his knock with a huge smile on her face. The smile faded to be replaced with one not quite so warming. She was dressed up as if going out. Rocky apologized for stopping by without warning but had wanted to talk to Joe for a moment. "Sorry, Joes at work at the garage. He'll be home around nine." She invited him in but the invitation lacked sincerity, whoever she had anticipated it wasn't himself. Rocky thanked her but said he had to get home to dinner. Raising his cap he turned and walked down the street. The sheriffs car passed him at the corner and headed back the direction Rocky had come from.

Rocky pulled the picture of the broach out of his pocket and stopped mid stride. On the dress Mrs. Steckler was wearing was it's twin. Rocky turned and stopped again as he saw the Sheriffs car in front of the Steckler's home. Rocky broke into a run thinking something might be wrong there but skidded to a halt as he saw Lester approach the door with a bouquet of flowers in his hand. Rocky got his pocket notebook out and made a few remarks. Instead of heading home he went back into town to the garage. Joe was in the process of replacing a muffler. He got Rocky a Coke and sat him comfortably while he finished. Half an hour later he stripped out of his overall and washed his hands. "Let's head over to Murphy's for beer and a sandwich."

In the cool atmosphere of the dim bar they sat with a beer and corned beef on rye each. Joe took a bite and savored the beef, mustard and rye. By the look on his face Joe was in rapture. Rocky grinned as he bit into his own. "Damn good sandwiches they have here." Joe nodded agreement. Rocky pulled out the picture and laid it on the table. "Joe, I hate to bring you back to earth but we need to talk. Did you ever see this broach in any of your mom's jewelry." Joe looked at the picture and then brought out a picture from his wallet. "Now you mention it she did." He handed over his mom and dads wedding picture and sure enough it was on her wedding dress. "Dad had to send off for it. She used to say it cost him a months wages." "Did she ever lose it?" "Yeah a long time ago but I guess she found it last year. She only wears it once in a while." Rocky made the sound usually spelt tsk tsk.

"Joe how does your mom feel about Sheriff Lester?" "What do ya think, she can't stand him." "Joe, I saw him not an hour ago talking to your mother. He brought her flowers, and she was dressed to the nines and expecting him." Joes face turned crimson, his hands started shaking. "She can't stand him." He repeated but his voice suddenly lacked conviction. "Joe are you sure that she found the broach and that it wasn't a gift." "you mean from Lester?" Rocky nodded. He hadn't want to say the name as it seemed to inflame Joe. "Rocky you say you saw him at our place, if anyone else had told me that I'd a punched them into next week and called them a liar. You're a straight shooter though and if you say you saw them then I guess you saw them." They spent quite a while talking and reasoning things out. Joe suddenly stood up, "I want to talk to the Sheriff." Rocky held up a hand, "Joe you can't go barging into the sheriff office and accuse Lester of something. He'll just trump up a reason to arrest you." Joe looked up in surprise. "I'm going to talk to the Sheriff not Lester."

They walked back to Sheriff Andrews place. Agnes opened the door and welcomed them warmly. She placed a hand on Rocky's arm. "Twice visiting in a week, I hope this becomes a habit." Rocky grinned. He had a soft spot for her and it was nice it was reciprocated. After he got this story wrapped up he would start visiting more often in a social way. "Sorry to say but we need to talk to your dad." She pouted at the news but went to get her father. Everyone was seated in the living room and after bringing in coffee and cakes Agnes sat near Rocky.

Joe held out a hand for Rocky's picture. The picture passed from Rocky to Joe to Andrews. Joe took charge of the conversation. "Sheriff, have you ever seen this broach before. Sheriff Andrew took out his glasses and carefully threaded them over his ears. He peered at the picture and a warm smile brightened his face. "Sure do, Lester bought it to give to his girl. Her that was killed while I was out of town. Cost him a packet too." He looked again at the picture and saw the cloth with a splotch on it. "Where'd you find this?" he asked sitting up and leaning towards them. "I was doing some metal detecting and found it where the six trees circle. It's pretty filled in now but a long time ago it would have been pretty wide open" The sheriff reached for the phone. Rocky held it fast. "Not so fast sheriff, we think Lester might be involved." "That's a pretty provocative statement to be made on such slim evidence." Joe and Rocky spelled out their idea and why they thought it. The sheriff listened and took notes. "You two wouldn't be coming to me unless you had an idea of how to get a confession and wanted me to hear it. Much as I hate to think ill of Lester I think you're on the right track and I'll go through with it." He got up and Agnes helped him on with his coat. "I'm going too, an extra set of ears just makes the case that much stronger." The men would have objected but the look on Agnes's face left no doubt she was going along."

A block away from the house, Joe gave them some information on listening places that could used and out of sight of anyone in the living room. In case of emergency there was a shed that locked from the inside and a small tree house. "why should the shed lock from the inside?" Agnes asked. Joe grinned, "Sometimes I'd get pissed off and go in there and mope. It was my place where no one could bother me. Not much in it but some old rusty tools though." Agnes looked up at her father. "In case of emergency I'll take the tree house and you can scoot into the shed." Her father lowered his brows, "So who made you in charge?" She patted his stomach, "He did, there isn't a way in hell you could climb up a tree and fit into a small tree house." Joe and Rocky went ahead with Agnes and Morgan waiting until everyone was inside.

Sheriff Morgan peered through the kitchen into the living room. Seated on the dilapidated couch were Joe and Rocky. Mrs. Steckler was serving sodas then sat down with a cup of coffee. Rocky pulled out his picture of the broach. Looking up he noticed that it was not on her dress now. He laid it on the table and opened his soda. As he drank he kept a side eye on Mrs. Steckler. Her curiosity got the better of her and she reached over and pulled the picture closer. Her sharp intake of breath was heard even by the ears of Sheriff Morgan and Agnes. "where'd you find this." Joe was startled by the change in his mom's face. "I was doing some metal detecting and found it in the ground near where the lady was found." Mrs. Stecklers face turned a dark red. "She weren't no lady, She was a hussy if there ever was one. A jezebel, that's what she was. That was my pin and she got it off your dad. He took it from me to give to her!" there was venom in her voice and she spat the words out. "She was stepping out with my husband while she was seeing that nice Deputy Lester."

Joe looked with shock at his mother, "Ma, that pin was given to her by Deputy Lester, Sheriff Morgan said he saved up a long time to get it." Mrs. Steckler narrowed her eyes. "But Lester said your dad gave it to her, He said he saw her messing about with other men including your dad, he was so upset about it made me mad." She reached over and picked up the phone. Joe and Rocky had no doubts about who she was calling. "Hank, can you come over?" she asked plaintively, over the ear piece she heard his affirmative answer.

Morgan and Agnes saw through the curtain when the Squad car arrived. Morgan pulled Agnes towards the tree as he headed for the shed. Sheriff Hank Lester stomped around the house, tested the shed door, even going so far as to climb up and look in the tree house. Everything seemed clear but the tone of Mrs Stecklers voice had made him cautious. As he entered in the back door Morgan slid out of the shed and Agnes climbed down out of the tree house. "How'd he miss you, He looked right in?" Agnes suppressed her laughter. I was up in the roof with hands and feet on all four walls, just like I used to do when I hid in your closet to scare you!" Back to the curtain they saw Lester walk in the house as if he owned the place. Seeing Rocky and Joe he stopped and looked over at Mrs. Steckler. She was shaking. "These two giving you a hard time? I'll take care of it." Mrs. Steckler shook her head. "They found her broach, the one I ripped off her blouse after you knocked her out." Lester looked at her quizzically, "Now you see, you shouldn't open your mouth." "You said Joseph gave it to her but the Sheriff said you did." Lester smiled, "So I did, but she was going around with everyone so I thought I'd get done with the little tramp. You were a big help, just like you're going to help me now." Mrs Steckler looked startled and Joe and Rocky looked out side the front window as if seeking help."

Lester pulled out a gun and pointed at the three. He turned to Rocky, "I guess I have you to thank for clearing up all the loose ends. Oh, I checked around the house and there wasn't a soul around. Nobody comes this way often so we'll just have a nice chat before I take you out, I wouldn't want to dirty up the place. Betty works real hard to keep this dump presentable. Betty was crying into a handkerchief. "It wasn't Joseph, he was true to me and you made me think he wasn't." Lester laughed, "Of course, it got you madder than spit and you even helped with the details to get him good and fried. Much obliged, I'm sure." Joe jumped to his feet as Lester cocked his gun. "You killed my pa, DAMN YOU!" A swift kick at the door and Sheriff Morgan was inside and had Lester's gun before he could fire. Agnes came in and had Betty in an iron hold as she tried to claw Agnes off. "Guess we've heard enough to get this to court. Agnes when we get done you write down everything you heard, I'll do the same.

Rocky was not only at the courthouse to cover the trial but was a witness alongside the Sheriff and Agnes as well as Joe. The prosecutor had cut a deal with Mrs. Lester and her testimony was almost enough on its own to hang Lester. Rocky's account of the trial made interesting reading as he gave full color to the story. Lester was given life in prison without possibility of parole. Mrs. Steckler received 15 years. Sheriff Morgan took back his job as sheriff full time and Joe went back to working at the garage plus worked with Morgan to become a deputy. It meant long hours but kept his mind off his family problems. Agnes and Rocky are seeing each other steady and both are very happy. Oh, Rocky is on the way to Star Reporter!

DID YOU HEAR THAT?

Rocky was seated behind his desk, his hat pushed back as became a newsman of his caliber. He finished off the last sentence in his report regarding the trial of Sheriff Joe Lester and Betty Steckler. Dropping it into the ready bin he looked up at the board for anything of interest. The phones were quiet and it seemed as if crime in this small backwater town was on holiday. He dropped in the editor's office announcing he was going to walk around and see if he could dig up a story somewhere.

Out on the street he buttoned up his pea coat and lit his pipe in the shelter of the doorframe. As he strolled the streets like a bloodhound, his rapid puffs made a steam train trail drifting off behind him. He dropped into the Cup of Joe Diner on Market Street. The coffee was worthy of the name, and he might hear something in the crowded diner to get him a story. Looking the place over he chose a stool at the end of the counter. Behind him were two out of towners. They looked up at Rocky and promptly stopped talking.

Rocky ordered a large breakfast and coffee. Once the order was given he placed a headphone over his ears and brought out a small portable radio. He rocked gently to whatever he was listening too, his mouth forming words to a song. After a look at Rocky the two men felt comfortable talking again assuming he probably couldn't hear them. Rocky had them fooled, he hadn't turned on the radio.

Acting as if he was listening to music Rocky relaxed and ate his breakfast. Behind him the men recommenced their conversation "Roy, I don't know if we should get rid of this one here." The man addressed as Roy looked astonished. "Why the hell not? Plenty of places around, small town with only a hick town sheriff and maybe a deputy at most. We get rid of this one here and our problems are solved. Hank will let us know where to pick up the next one through the usual channels. Look Tom, we've already had to hold on to it longer than expected. Now the body is starting to deteriorate and fluids are going to come out. It smells terrible and we're not going to be able to hide things much longer. We get rid of it quick then beat hell out of town. We do it right and nobody will know anything until were home and dry." Tom didn't look completely convinced but shrugged and slurped his coffee.

Finishing his breakfast Rocky thought about the possibilities of their conversation. It sounded as if they were dropping of a body and hoping no one would find it. He looked at the napkin holder and adjusted it slightly to get a better look at the men. Both had a hardened look about them though Roy seemed to be more astute as well as being smoother. He contemplated following them himself, he considered himself brave enough but not stupid enough. Rocky finished up and headed over to the sheriff's house. Leave it to the professionals. He wanted to discuss what he had heard with him.

Agnes opened the door with a warm smile. As a close friend she was always ready to welcome Rocky. Granted, she was sometimes perturbed when he wanted to see her father rather than her. She recognized by the look on his face that he had come to see the sheriff part of her father. Escorting Rocky into a chair across from the sheriff she placed a breakfast and coffee in front of Rocky. He looked at Agnes in alarm but the warm sweet smile and the hand on his arm were eloquent. He'd have to eat a second breakfast and drink his eighth coffee.

As they ate Rocky explained what he had heard and thought about it. Sheriff Morgan put his cup down and considered what Rocky said. "I'm surprised you heard them unless you were close by, even then you'd have thought they'd have kept their voices down." Rocky pulled out his radio and headphones. "I had these on my ears but didn't put on the radio. They figured I couldn't hear so kept on with the conversation."

Morgan playfully punched Rocky on the shoulder. "Excellent thinking, you'd make a good detective if you ever want to give up reporting." He got up and strolled to the front room phone. "Cooper, you got something on right now? Good, I want you to take the car and look for two men, they look like out of towners in black suits and hats. Find out what they're up to. On second thought, bring the car here and pick me up. I don't like the sound of this. What, well o.k. but I'll have the radio on here in case you need backup. You go careful hear!" He came back into the kitchen and recommenced his breakfast but with his mind elsewhere.

Agnes reached over and turned on the radio and leaned on Rocky's back to whisper in his ear. Morgan looked up when Rocky finally let out a snicker and spilled some of his coffee. He opened his mouth to say something but was stopped by a squelch from the radio. "Found them sheriff, they were selling a used auto. Sold it to Mrs. Murphy on Arnold Street. Everything seems o.k. I did a check of the car and it's a bit beat up but runs o.k.. I don't see anything that we need to hold them on." Sheriff Morgan had Cooper head back to the office. "Looks like a bum steer. Seems like they're just out here selling. Figured a small town would be easier to sell a beat up junker than in the city.

Mrs. Murphy dropped by to show Agnes her new car. She called in through the screen door before opening it and letting herself in. "Agnes! I've finally got a car! Now you won't have to pick me up for church in the police car. Never did look good having the police car outside so often." She giggled into her hands, "Folks were getting the idea I was doing something I oughtn't." Agnes went out with Rocky accompanying. He looked the vehicle over, under and inside and decided it was a decent car for short hops. Even if it was dented and a little rusted" When he got to the trunk though he wrinkled up his nose.

"There's a God-awful stink coming from the back here." Mrs. Murphy nodded knowingly. "They explained that they used the car for carrying back deer from hunting and had a small one in it for a while they forgot about. The smell should go away after a few days." She opened the trunk and though empty gave off the lingering smell of putrefaction. It assailed their nostrils and made them gag. Rocky pulled out a handkerchief and covered mouth and nose. He rummaged around in the trunk, running his hand around and lifting the carpet and wood underneath to take a look at the spare tire well. Mrs. Murphy promptly fainted.

Sheriff Morgan hurried outside at the sound of commotion. Rocky showed him the cause. In the well in the trunk was the swollen remains of someone who had died at least five days ago. Blood and other liquids were coming out of the mouth, nose and ears. Morgan went inside to call the state police in on the case. He also called Cooper to come over to the house. When Cooper arrived, he was privately given a dressing down due to the shoddy inspection he claimed to have done. When shown the remains in the trunk he turned a sickly green. The state police arrived within an hour. The remains were removed, and the car impounded. Mrs. Murphy was distraught at losing her money and car all in the same day.

Rocky sat on the porch and wrote up his story with Agnes peering over his shoulder and making suggestions. Rocky closed his notebook so suddenly that Agnes thought she was irritating him and rose to retreat hastily inside. Rocky lashed out a hand and caught her wrist and brought her back. Agnes looked over her shoulder at Mrs. Murphy as Rocky made his thoughts known.

Not long after Agnes and Rocky were seated in Ralphs Pretty Good Car Deals. Seated behind his desk Ralph senior listened to Rocky's proposal. "Such a shame, Mrs. Murphy hasn't had a lot of luck lately. Let's take a walk outside and look some over. Agnes, you pick out the one you think she'd like then we'll all drive it over and hand her the keys. As they walked around Rocky wrote his notes for the write up he promised regarding the sympathetic gift Ralph was giving. It was good advertisement for Ralph and another story for Rocky. Plus, there was the benefit to Mrs. Murphy.

Agnes picked out a decent 1959 Buick LeSabre Hardtop. It was in good condition with seventy thousand miles and would last a long time if she maintained it. Rocky thought about checking in with Joe and seeing if he'd be willing to keep an eye on it. He finished the writeup in the back seat while they drove back to Agnes's home. Sure enough Mrs. Murphy was still there and still upset. Rocky did a quick check on his camera as Agnes leapt out of the car before Ralph had brought it to a stop. She practically dragged Mrs. Murphy out as Ralph stood by with keys outstretched and Rocky took pictures. Her tears flowed once more as she hugged everyone including a couple who happened to be walking by. Before driving off though she did a check of the trunk and was relieved to find only a spare tire there. Sheriff Morgan praised Rocky and Agnes on their idea then went back inside to nap. Rocky suggested a light lunch somewhere which delighted Agnes.

The diner was packed. Rocky and Agnes had to squeeze in with couple of old men having a chat over open face sandwiches. As they ate, they made small talk and tried to ignore the men. Ignoring them became difficult as the men began debating. "I'm telling you Fred it was this long." He held his hands approximately six inches apart. Fred scoffed and putting down his coffee he held his hands about three inches apart. "And I say it was only this big, I ought to know, I saw it when it was in his hands" The first man bit into his sandwich and spoke while still chewing, "It only looked that small because Hanks got big hands." Fred pulled a picture out of his shirt pocket and shoved it before his friend's face. "Look down at his belt buckle and you'll see how big it was. His hands right down there and wrapped around it."

Agnes choked on her mashed potatoes. Rocky was about to try and get the men to stop talking but Agnes was silently laughing and shaking her head. She went white then a deep red when Frank pulled the picture back and put it before her, "Look at this here and tell me how big you think that is."

Rocky's hand leapt across grabbing the picture and was about to rip it up when his eye was caught by the view. Laughing he handed it back to the man who again showed it to Agnes. Blushing she looked to see a man in waders and in his lowered hand was a small fish.

Finishing their lunch they took a walk to the park and sat for a while. The only other occupants were two boys in the sandbox. Over the peace and quiet of the park they heard them talking.

"I heard your dad beat you yesterday." The boy he was speaking to shrugged. "Yeah he usually beats me a couple of times a week." The first boy looked up concerned, "You want I should help you?" The other shrugged again, "It won't make a difference." Rocky looked over concerned. Agnes was listening as well but didn't seem to consider it a problem. He considered that odd knowing her heart. One of the boys pointed down the street. "Your dads coming," The boy looked over and saw a tall man carrying a wooden box. He was walking quickly towards the park. The boy looked up and brushed himself off as he stood. "Time for a beating." He passed by Rocky and was halted by his outstretched hand.

"Look kid, I'm friends with the sheriff, if your dad's beating you, I can get you help." The child pulled his arm away and ran towards the approaching man. Rocky and Agnes could see him pointing and gesturing towards them. The man approached with long strides. Rocky rose to meet him. The man stopped a yard away looking at Rocky speculatively. "I hear you threatened to go to the sheriff and complain that I'm beating my son." Rocky came a step closer, "You think beating him is right?" The man shrugged which made Rocky start to burn.

Only Agnes's hand on his arm prevented him from taking a more active stance. The man brought forward the box, "Look, I'm just teaching the kid chess, he's good but I am not just going to just let him win. If he wins, he's earned it. I can't see why the sheriff should have anything to say about it." Rocky stammered out an apology and sat down next to Agnes who was shaking with laughter.

Moments later the sheriff's car approached. Parking outside the gate Sheriff Morgan got out and sat on the bench next to them. "Rocky, it's a good thing you kept your wits about you. I got a feeling you were tempted to follow those two around and see what they were up to for yourself. He pulled a fax from his pocket. Those two were bad news." He looked up from his notes," You ever hear of Lucky Luciano?" Rocky nodded, who hadn't? Apparently, they were two of his group's delivery boys. What the hell they thought they were doing though I haven't a clue. They were supposed to just dump the body somewhere and scoot. Instead, they picked up the body in the vehicle where you saw it and were driving around for a few days. Seems they forgot it was back there until it started to smell. Then they figured they could dump the whole thing and make a couple of bucks at the same time."

Rocky shook his head. If this was the type organized crime was recruiting nowadays then crime should be wiped out within a month. Agnes kissed Rocky goodbye and got into the squad car with her father. Rocky headed back to the paper to put in his stories. On the way he stopped at the jewelers for a ring. He was feeling it was time to solidify things between Agnes and himself.

Also by David Booker

Time Is
Time Is
Time Is, Time Was
Time Is, Time Was, Time Will Be
Time Is Once More
Time Is Lost
Time Is Changing
Time Is Passing

Standalone
The Reluctant Left Hand of God
Artistic Endeavors
A Glimpse of My Shorts
Another Glimpse Of My Shorts
A Mystery In My Pocket

Watch for more at https://timeiswaswillbe.wordpress.com/.

About the Author

David Booker is an author who wiill try his hand at numerous styles. Short stories, mysteries, humor, horror, time travel and rants he enjoys a constant challenge. With a seven book series under the Time Is banner to A Glimpse of My Shorts and Another Glimpse he churns out books regularly.

Read more at https://timeiswaswillbe.wordpress.com/.

www.ingramcontent.com/pod-product-compliance
Lightning Source LLC
Chambersburg PA
CBHW050528160726

48003CB00002B/505